LET'S NOT SUGAR COAT IT

REAL, RAW, & UNFILTERED STORIES WITHOUT THE BS!

Volume One

Soul Spark
— PUBLISHING —

Soul Spark Publishing
An imprint of Soul Spark Enterprises
soulsparkpublishing.com

This is a work of nonfiction. Nevertheless, some names, identifying details, or characteristics of individuals have been changed. Additionally, certain people who have been listed are composites of a number of individuals and their experiences.

This publication is designed to provide accurate and authoritative information in regard to the subject matter covered. It is sold with the understanding that neither the author nor the publisher is engaged in rendering legal, investment, accounting, medical, or other professional services. While the publisher and author have used their best efforts in preparing this book, they make no representations or warranties with respect to the accuracy or completeness of the contents of this book and specifically disclaim any implied warranties of merchantability or fitness for a particular purpose. No warranty may be created or extended by sales representatives or written sales materials. The advice and strategies contained herein may not be suitable for your situation. You should consult with a professional when appropriate. Neither the publisher nor the author shall be liable for any loss of profit or any other commercial damages, including but not limited to special, incidental, consequential, personal, or other damages.

Let's Not Sugarcoat It: Real, Raw, & Unfiltered Stories Without the BS! Volume One,
First edition 2024
ISBN 978-1-964445-04-5 (paperback) 978-1-964445-02-1 (ebook)

Book Cover and Interior Formatting and Styling by Lucie Ward
Graphic icon by Christos Georghiou
Editing by Michelle Ireland

To anyone with an untold story to share.

Table of Contents

NOTE TO READER

The stories in this book are shared with deep vulnerability, humility, and a great sense of care for you, the reader. As you journey through these pages, you may encounter themes of trauma and hardship. While we have not gone into graphic detail, some stories may still evoke strong emotions. We encourage you to approach this book with compassion for yourself, and to ground yourself as needed.

Some chapters may stir discomfort or be emotionally activating. So please, honor your feelings—whether that means pausing, skipping a chapter, or taking a break before returning. We've included content guidance at the start of each chapter to help you decide if you'd like to continue reading. Should you feel activated, we trust you to seek the support you need.

These stories are gifts we have chosen to share with you. We trust you'll find the wisdom and messages meant for you within each one.

Preface

Welcome, you badass reader! You hold in your hands not just a book, but a powerful collection of voices that are ready to resonate with your heart and soul.

Have you ever felt like life threw you curveballs? Or found yourself navigating the messy, unpredictable waters of your existence? Well, then you're landed in the right place.

We're Alex and Bella, the dynamic duo behind the <u>Let's Not Sugarcoat It Podcast</u>. We've made it our mission to engage in genuine, unfiltered conversations that cut through the noise. Our brand is built on the belief that through sharing our own trials and triumphs, we're better able to foster real connections and create a community where everyone feels seen, heard, and understood. Our passion shines through on every page of this book, and is a testament to our commitment to authenticity.

In this book, you'll discover the courageous and unfiltered stories of nineteen remarkable authors, each bravely sharing their truth. These aren't everyday tales of triumph; they're raw accounts of hardship, resilience, and the messy beauty of overcoming adversity. Each narrative offers a unique perspective that might echo your own experiences—whether it's grappling with a personal challenge, confronting fears, or chasing dreams that feel just out of reach.

So, why should you continue on and read this book? Because it's a lifeline. A reminder that you're not alone in your struggles. Each story is meant to offer you a hand and light the path towards healing and connection. Our vision is that you'll be inspired to pick this book up, flip to any page, and find something that resonates with you, something that might give you the encouragement you need at that exact moment.

Let's be real: life can be pretty f*cking brutal at times. That's why the key is to cut through the BS and embrace the truth. It's in these authentic conversations that healing occurs, community is forged, and we discover the strength to keep moving forward.

Buckle up and prepare for a journey through the hearts and minds of these amazing authors. You're not just a reader—you're part of a bigger conversation. We hope you enjoy the ride!

Alex & Bella

SENSITIVITY ADVISORY

The following chapters may include topics that are sensitive to readers. The authors are sharing their personal experiences with abuse, death, addiction, trauma, and suicide. While the details of these experiences are not explicit and are told from a perspective of healing and hindsight, please prioritize your own mental well-being when enjoying this book.

Foreword

Let's talk about belief, specifically the human belief system. I would argue that this belief system is the pivotal foundation of our being. The antecedent propelling us to our respective destinations, wherever it may lead, through the endless possibilities that exist when we enter this world. It can lead us to seemingly impossible heights. Yet, ironically, it is quite often our most formidable foe.

Most of us are born with an innate ability to dream. To believe we can become anything we want in this life. But this gift eventually becomes threatened by many different factors—trauma, injury, mental health challenges, self doubt, and the protection of limiting beliefs that slowly grow their venomous roots as we age.

I was a hockey player for the first thirty years of my life. Like many kids, I dreamt of playing in the NHL—the best league in the world. But I made the same mistake so many of us make. Around age thirteen, I started putting governors on my dream; the roots of my own limiting beliefs started to spread. I believed I was good, but not that good. Certainly not NHL good. I was cut from different select teams, was never going to be drafted, and was never going to sniff the highest levels of junior hockey. So, not letting naivety get the best of me, I identified a new dream—the NCAA. I figured if I could get a scholarship to play college hockey, that would be pretty damn sweet. That would be my NHL. Since I wasn't the most skilled player, I had to fight my way, literally, into Tier II Junior hockey. I barely snuck onto the Vernon Vipers of the British Columbia Hockey League (BCHL) through my hard hitting style, and fighting everyone in sight.

But even this smaller dream was in jeopardy after a horrific accident. I was lit on fire at a team camping trip when a gas and bonfire stunt went horribly wrong. I was a reckless young man. I thought I was invincible, always doing stupid shit for attention, adrenaline, and feeding my young ego. I was also living up to my fighter stereotype, labeled as the wild child from Revelstoke, BC.

After the fire was put out, the nightmare began. I sat on a cooler at the party, ass-naked as there was nothing left of my clothing from the blaze, bleeding, filthy, charred, and in complete shock. My skin had melted into piles in various spots on my body. Like a giant candle had been liquefied and poured all over me. And the smell. The smell of burnt flesh is something that stays etched in your memory forever. A panic ensued, as everyone knew I needed to get to a hospital. We couldn't call 911 since we were out in the bush with no cell service. After the most painful forty minutes of my life en route to the hospital, I was put to sleep, wrapped like a mummy, and airlifted to Vancouver General Hospital. I was eventually told by doctors, gavel in hand, that I would spend the next few months in the burn unit and that my hockey career was over. Recovery from second and third degree burns to forty percent of your body is no joke.

I listened to the doctors. They were experts after all. I accepted my fate and figured I could still lead a relatively normal life as a burn survivor, and not a hockey player. But as the weeks of physical and mental torture passed, something magical happened. A simple phone call from my coach with the Vernon Vipers. He had been talking with another coach from Brown University in the NCAA. They were looking for a guy that could put the fear of god in the defenseman of the Ivy League. Well, I was great at that. Next thing I knew I was on the phone with this coach from Brown. I was almost twenty years old, with one more year of junior hockey eligibility, and had never talked to an NCAA coach up until this moment in my life. I was so close, and there I was, mummified in the burn unit. My body was in ruins and I'd be bedridden for months.

After my parents hung up the phone in my room in the burn unit, I started asking myself questions. *They're telling me I won't be able to play hockey in a few months. Why? Why does it have to be over?*

And believe me, there was a very respectable, long list of reasons why. Infection risk was very high. The skin grafts were going to be very limiting and painful. My recovery would take two years. I wouldn't be able to sweat from the large grafted areas on my legs and torso. I would have to wear a bodysuit for the full two years. And, I was likely to still be in the burn unit when my last season of junior hockey started.

This was the pivotal moment where I reclaimed my dream of the NCAA, and I was willing to protect it with my life. I was truly willing to die before giving up. Based on the aforementioned list of all the reasons why my hockey career was over, I thought they were telling me that because it was going to hurt too much. But the pain of giving up on this dream would be far greater than any physical pain I would endure in the coming years.

Today, I am a Cognitive Performance and Visualization Coach, as well as a best selling author and international speaker. People often ask me how I discovered visualization. This is how. I was bedridden in a burn unit and my body was out of commission. My mind was all I had. And once I made this promise to myself that I would go to Brown or die trying, I tapped into the most powerful resource we possess as human beings—the power of our mind. I unlocked this superpower through visualization. I was able to re-lay the foundation of my broken belief system and all those limiting beliefs I'd been protecting over the years and rediscover what I was truly capable of.

After five years of setbacks, multiple surgeries, and physical pain that would test my belief system daily, I was in the NHL. Which, by the way, I still never even thought of until I was twenty-four years old. Another example of me limiting myself, but again, when that dream was reclaimed, I protected it with my life and went to work on a new mind movie through my visualization practice. During my journey to get back on the ice after my burn injury, I wanted to give up at some point every single day, but that vision I projected at the back of my brain's big screen TV was too vivid, too powerful. Deep down I believed to my core that I was capable of what I was envisioning.

Interestingly, life after hockey was the hardest time in my life. I hit rock bottom after a career ending neck surgery while playing in the NHL. I faced a loss of identity, traumatic child births, divorce, my dad was diagnosed with ALS, and I had no purpose in life. All in a span of under two years. My mental health was threatened because I was playing the victim and allowing adversity and trauma to poison my belief system—the belief, or lack thereof, that something else was out there for me.

In my darkest, rock bottom moment, I sought help from a counselor. This was not an easy thing for me to do, especially as a man conditioned to never show weakness in the hockey world. Thankfully, through her help, I came to an important realization—there are many pillars that make up our mental health system. There is certainly a physical component, and I was really good at overcoming physical adversity. Through my burn injury, and my role as a fighter in hockey, I was physically tough. If you put a wall in front of me, and there is something I want on the other side of that wall, I will break through that fucking wall to get what I want. But there are also emotional and spiritual components to mental health. And in that regard, I was just an immature little boy inside, and I didn't know how to deal with that kind of adversity. I couldn't physically fight it. As soon as I started going to work on a new mind movie, not as Aaron Volpatti the hockey player, but the Aaron Volpatti I am today, along with incorporating the emotional and spiritual elements, my life changed dramatically again.

Visualization has not only gotten me out of the burn unit to come back and play hockey when I was told that it wasn't possible. It also got me to Brown University and later propelled me to the NHL. But most importantly, it saved my life after hockey.

Adversity is truly a gift. Every piece of greatness I've achieved in my life, both professionally and personally, has always been preceded by extreme adversity. I know now that this is no accident. Because we don't fortify our belief system when our life is easy, we build it up during the most difficult times in our life. The real struggle is the ability to reframe it this way. It is a skill that is perfected through the hard shit. Living, believing, and protecting our vision of what we want in our lives; who we want to become. We are all on our own unique journey. There is no right path, only your path. And what I know for certain is that it is the paths less traveled that lead us to greatness- whatever that means to you. We must struggle. We must go through what feels like hell. It is a prerequisite for an untouchable belief system.

Aaron Volpatti

The power comes in the choosing.

CHAPTER 1

Things Are Not Always What They Seem

Izabela Picco

We receive so many mixed messages .... Be strong and independent, but not too strong. Follow your dreams, but only after you take care of everyone else's needs first. Voice your opinion but only if it fits the narrative. Society says; you are a woman, you can do all things. But you're already doing everything. We're exhausted leaving no space to do the things we really want to do. We give and we give and we give until somewhere along the way we lose ourselves entirely.

So let me tell you a story, a story of how I lost everything, a story of how I burned my old life down and rose like a phoenix from the ashes. A story of coming home to myself.

In the beginning there was me. I always wanted to start a story this way: a young immigrant girl from Poland who came with her parents to find a better life in Canada.

Like any traditional immigrant family I worked the family business from the time I was thirteen. I'm the only child and therefore everything fell to me. Let's just say I was the only egg in the basket. My parents taught me to be strong and independent at a young age. Not necessarily by choice but by the situations we were in, I needed to grow up very quickly. But, I questioned everything and went against the grain. I was a non-conformist in a culture where that wasn't allowed for women. My father loved me dearly and allowed me certain freedoms when I was younger. He was my biggest cheerleader. He supported me in any crazy idea I had, even bought me my first camera for my photography business that I started at 19. However, my independent, non-conformist nature became a problem as I got older.

Culturally the roles of women were clearly defined. Women are the supporting act, they don't rock the boat, they don't go out without their man, they stay with the kids, and don't talk back. Well let me tell you, talk back I did.

I got my first taste of where I belonged on the totem pole of life in my culture when my cousin started working the family business and got paid two dollars more per hour than I did—just for being a man. I had worked in the business for more than two years and he just swooped in and got paid more. I didn't think it was fair, but it was the family business, and I had no choice or say in the matter. I struggled with the mixed messages; I felt the injustice. Why was I worth less just because I was a woman?

Our family left Poland for Austria in 1988 as refugees to escape communism and I found myself having a completely different childhood. My parents worked long hours and I was often left to my own devices, learning my independence that way. We lived in a hotel room for a year, and then moved to a room in a farmhouse for the second year.

When we immigrated to Canada I learned the language sooner and needed to help with grownup things. I learned about what it took to run a business and the sacrifice you must make in order to be successful. I was allowed to follow my dreams, buy what I wanted, go where I wanted, but only if the men approved. I remember having to get glasses in my early teens. I wanted smaller lenses but ended up getting the biggest frames they had because my dad thought I looked best in them. They were so big that when I smiled the frames touched mid-cheek bone and pushed up past half of my forehead. When it came to buying my first car I couldn't even pick the make or model I wanted. I was paying for it, but because I was a girl they, the men in my life, said I didn't know anything about cars and they knew best. <eyeroll>

Things have changed since then. Our time in Canada influenced my parents to change some of their beliefs, however my upbringing was centered around those beliefs and messages. I often rebelled, but was quickly brought back with guilt and shame. I questioned everything—am I free to follow my dreams or do I need to ask permission? Is it the right thing for me or is it the right thing for everyone else? The constant back and forth was exhausting, the constant questioning of what I truly wanted versus what I was supposed to be and do. I didn't know what to do with these questions that often went unanswered. There were no self-development talks back then with my family or friends, things were the way they always were and I was not to question anything.

But there was a void inside me and it grew deeper and deeper. I didn't understand why I was feeling this way, why I was wanting more. I look back now and think, man, was I ever like Belle from Beauty and the Beast, wanting more than that provincial life. On the outside I had everything going for me and yet I wasn't happy. I started to convince myself that this was the way it was supposed to be. Over the years, the pressure grew to be someone I was not. This way of being led me into an unhealthy long-term relationship where I continued to push the envelope against the control people had over me. I started rebelling again.

I remember one day my boyfriend and I were going to the club and I wore a thong under my skirt. My ex told me that I wasn't allowed to wear thongs to the bar and ripped them off me. He then proceeded to give me his boxer shorts so I could put them on before we went out. I put those damn briefs on, went to the bar, proceeded to the bathroom and took them off. I threw those suckers in the garbage and danced the night away commando, a silent yet deliberate FU*K you to the control he was trying to have over me. Because my ex was from my culture and had his own insecurities, the relationship turned verbally and physically abusive in the end. I wanted to leave way sooner, but if I left it would break up friendships, the families, and the future we were building "together."

No one was thinking of me, not even me. That way of thinking would be "selfish" and that's not how women are supposed to be. "You've already invested so many years, why would you leave," they asked. No one saw the things that happened behind closed doors because I was ashamed. Ashamed for not living my truth and ashamed that it was so bad. I kept my mouth shut and pretended to be someone I wasn't. The light inside me continued to dim, and the void continued to grow. Yet I stayed. I stayed for eight and half years because I was telling myself I should; it's the right thing to do. I stayed because I thought I needed to stay. I stayed because I didn't trust who I was. I stayed to please my parents and friends. I stayed because I didn't have my voice. I didn't know I could choose myself. Every time I said no when I wanted to say yes, every time I said yes when I wanted to say no, every time I chose someone else's needs over my own, I heard a whisper. A whisper that told me that there is more to this life.

I know that I'm not alone in this. So many of us are given mixed messages from the time we are born, never feeling like we are enough. Be independent but not too independent, be a super mom that attends all school functions, but also have a stellar career. Be assertive but don't ask for too much. The list goes on and on. So many dreams go unrealized because we sacrifice so much for others.

I started to feel trapped. I felt like a caged bird, a bird that had her wings clipped, a bird that wanted to tear everything apart if you got too close. The more I felt trapped the more I wanted to be free. At one point I felt so empty and depleted that I just shut down for a while. I suddenly stopped caring about what others wanted. I got curious about what life would look like alone, what would life look like if I was free from all the expectations. I finally reached my breaking point and broke out of that cage and left the relationship. I lost half my friends, I sold my condo, and I moved back home at the age of twenty-four. For the first time I didn't feel ashamed.

I will never forget the feeling; the feeling you get when you make a choice that is aligned with who you are. The world suddenly felt bright again, and I was ready to fly. No one was going to tell me what to do anymore! For the first time in my life, I felt my true essence. I started to get to know who I was. I wasn't afraid to take risks and I did whatever the hell I wanted. I was FREE! I had a successful business that took me all over the world, and my plans were to move out of the city to Europe as quickly as possible. My parents thought I was crazy, saying they didn't recognize who I was. Some of my girlfriends weren't allowed to hang out with me anymore because of their husbands' insecurities with their wives hanging out with a single woman, and at one point my parents asked me if I needed help because I was going out so much.

You see my parents weren't used to me going out alone without male supervision, and that made my dad especially uneasy. I didn't care. For the first time in my life I was living and breathing Bella. However, my self-discovery journey didn't last very long.

Ten months after my split with my ex I met Lee, my current husband. I didn't have enough time to find myself, I didn't have enough time to explore a world created by me for me. I didn't know that I had to start healing the trauma of my previous relationship before jumping into another one. We fell hard and fast for each other. Lee was completely different from my previous relationship, and I felt so safe and secure. I was very vocal on the things I didn't want in a relationship and in my life. However, what I forgot to do is speak the things I wanted into existence. I didn't want to stay in

Edmonton, I didn't want a traditional life, I didn't want him to work out of town, I didn't want to be alone. But slowly, year by year, I was getting everything I didn't want. I started to fall back into my old patterns, living into what I "should' do versus what felt aligned. We bought a house four months into our relationship because the market was going up, and everyone else was buying so we thought we should buy too. I'm sure you can remember a time in your life where suddenly everyone is getting together, getting married, and buying houses, the pressure is intense to keep up. Couples you thought would never marry, do because they get wrapped up in the peer pressure and societal expectations of what life is supposed to look like. The messaging from my family and friends was clear: you should get married soon because you're getting old and if you want children, you have to get on it. *You should do this, and you should do that! Who decides what you should do?*

We got married and soon after we started our fertility journey. The pressure to have children was very strong. I wasn't even sure yet I wanted children, but if I tried to voice that, I was met with shame and blame. How could I be so selfish? Our fertility journey lasted four years. We had beautiful identical twin girls, with the help of IVF, and I am grateful for them every second. On the outside we had the perfect life, everything that fairytales are made of. I had a wonderful husband, two kids, a beautiful home, and we traveled. What else could I possibly need? I fell into that trap of putting myself on the backburner, I stopped dreaming for myself. I was constantly doing things to make others happy. I wanted my husband to be successful in his career because I was already successful in mine. I felt that I needed to give him time to find himself because I snatched him up at a tender age of 21 and I was 25. *Although he will argue that part on who snatched who. And yes, I know what you are thinking ... I high-fived myself too.*

When we had kids, our circumstances changed because the girls came early, and I needed to be in the NICU with them. I took on the role of stay-at-home mom for a few years, but only after I experienced severe burnout. My husband wanted us to get a nanny right away, but I was living into those societal pressures of being a fantastic, well put together, always on time, house always clean, running two businesses, needing no help, kind of mom. The nanny came when the girls were 14 months old, but not without judgment. *I could write a whole book on the judgements in motherhood, but I guess I'll save that for another day.*

Let's Not Sugarcoat It

We continued living our lives according to "the plan." I slowly moved away from that passion and freedom I once felt and lived for during the brief time after I left my ex, and fell into the supporting role that was "meant" for me. Don't get me wrong, I did voice my dissatisfaction once in a while, only to be met with comments like "why can't you just be happy," "this is what life is," "be grateful for what you have," "stop chasing these unrealistic dreams." The thing is, no one asked me what I wanted.

I started to put my own desires on the back burner because I was now invested in my husband's career; I was there to support him. It was my job to keep the family together when he was out of town, work when it was convenient for his schedule, be available on his days off, and always be happy. We put him on a pedestal, and everything revolved around him. Now he never actually asked me to do that, but the way I was conditioned the expectation was there. I had done all the things I was supposed to for the 18 years we'd been together, but it didn't prevent my world from suddenly crumbling down beneath me.

I found myself in this place where the shock of our lifetime happened. My husband and I found my father's lifeless body on the bedroom floor in our house. This traumatic experience exposed the lack of connection we had over the last few years and all the ways we related to one another. You see, because I was living a life that wasn't by my design I made concessions for the ways I was feeling in my marriage. Everytime I felt lonely or sad, everytime I said yes when I meant no, every time I felt disconnected, I pushed the feeling away and told myself that I'm doing this, we are doing this, for us and our family. We both lived for each other but we never asked each other what it was that we wanted. We assumed we were doing what the other one needed. The lack of communication between us started to affect me more and more. The more I pushed for connection and communication the further we grew apart. We didn't understand then that we both brought unresolved childhood traumas into the relationship and a traumatic event, like the sudden death of my father, would bring it all to the surface.

My husband has always been cool, calm, and collected. That was his superpower. We learned recently, after several counseling sessions, about our attachment styles and how we deal with intense emotions. I leaned into intense emotions and my husband disassociated. The trauma of him having to do chest compressions on my father's lifeless body as we waited for the ambulance, pushed him deeper into emotional disassociation. I was busy planning and taking care of everything for the funeral, managing our children's emotions, being there for my mom, and pushing everything down. I was strong after all. I didn't know how to be vulnerable around him because I shut my feelings off. I felt disconnected. The distance between us didn't help. He worked out of town five days a week, home only for the weekends, and the constant visitors, who were coming to support us during this difficult time, didn't give us any space to connect with each other. He connected with someone else instead.

In one year I lost the two most important men in my life. When my husband left, I died a thousand deaths. I didn't know what was happening, I didn't understand what went wrong. I was doing all the "right" things. I lived for him. I gave up my life for him and now I was alone. My father was gone, and my husband left.

I started to hike. I couldn't keep all that emotion in my body anymore. I needed to process all the feelings instead of pushing shit down. I realized I'd been suppressing a lot of my feelings for many years. I finally woke up. It became more than just about him. It became about finding myself. I left a lot of tears and rage on that mountain, but man was my ass tight after that. I got curious about who I was. I admitted to myself how lonely I've been for so many years, and how I felt I wasn't good enough. I took responsibility for my part in the breakdown of our marriage but refused to accept some of the blame that wasn't mine to bear. I mourned my marriage and [hypothetically] burned that motherfucker down. I was an empty shell ready to surrender to the universe. I relinquished control and allowed things to flow through me. I tell you, this work isn't easy. For the first time in my life, I reached out to my community for support and accepted the help. No shame. I shared what I was going through and found that through the sharing I found peace. I started to choose myself unapologetically. I looked in the mirror and asked, "Who are you? Where have you been?"

The hardest part for me was letting go, not just of all the things we had created together, but all that I thought I needed to be in the process. Out of nothingness came the freedom of choice. I get to choose myself every day. I get to choose who I give my energy to. I get to choose how I move forward with my life. I get to choose how this phoenix rises. I am taking back my power and my gifts and pouring them back to me so I can show up as the best version of myself—the true version. And for that I am so grateful.

Let's Not Sugarcoat It

So, you all may think that my marriage ended, and it did for about two weeks. However there is a plot twist. Through this major breakdown came a major breakthrough. We just needed to give ourselves permission to burn it all down, let go of our old way of being, and own this rebirth. The "should" and "shouldn't" don't have the same merit. I still hear them all the time "you should leave him" or "you should stay for your children" but the difference now is that I get to choose. The power comes in the choosing.

I now own my choices and my life. I know who I am and I know what I want. This bird is out of the cage and she is never going back. Looking back at it now, it wasn't really about the men and their control; it was about living out of integrity and alignment. It was about giving my power away and living a life I didn't choose. Although on the outside it looked like I had everything anyone would want, things aren't always what they seem. As women we tend to put everyone's needs and happiness ahead of ourselves because we are conditioned that way from childhood. I was too young to realize that then, but I see it so clearly now. I'm a strong independent woman and I choose myself first. Always.

IZABELA PICCO

Izabela Picco embodies the spirit of serial entrepreneurship, launching her first venture at 19. With a background in marketing and design, her creative leadership drives every project, including The Picco Institute of Communication and Leadership Development and Lunar Skin. Currently, she oversees three thriving businesses in Kelowna, where she and her family have settled after a life of world travels. Izabela's ventures are platforms for growth, learning, and inspiration. As the co-host of the "Let's Not Sugar Coat It" podcast, she sparks thought-provoking conversations, demonstrating her talent for engaging and listening. Beyond business, Izabela's secret talent is making her children laugh on command, even in moments of frustration. Her personal life as a mother of twin girls and a partner in a nearly two-decade marriage enriches her understanding of leadership, emphasizing tenacity, empathy, and community—a people person at heart. You can find Izabela at info@letsnotsugarcoatit.com, thepiccoinstitute@gmail.com, and www.lunarskin.com.

Everything was uncertain, the future a vast unknown.

CHAPTER 2

No Matter What

Sanela Sehovac

I was ten years old and living in Montenegro when war broke out in the former Yugoslavia. This terrible conflict was divided between the Muslims, Catholics, and Christians. My parents came from differing beliefs so we felt at risk from all sides of conflict. My father, a Muslim, and my mother, a Christian, navigated a delicate balance during the war. They were never quite sure whom to trust, not even among family and friends. In a conflict where brother turned against brother, divided by faith, trust was a fragile commodity. At home, my parents shielded us from the turmoil outside, never speaking of the growing tension. They taught us that the world was divided not by religion, but by the simple distinction between good and bad people. Yet, outside our doors, the tension was palpable, a constant undercurrent in our lives.

When I was in the fifth grade, I had a teacher who had lost her son in the war. She took her grief and anger out on me, a young girl who just happened to have a Muslim father. For years, she bullied me relentlessly. Math was my favorite subject, and I excelled at it. But each year, she would fail me, forcing me to endure summer tutoring. The tutor, puzzled by the situation, would tell my parents that there was nothing more he could teach me—my math skills were already excellent, and I even ended up assisting him in tutoring other children.

In Montenegro at that time, only fifteen percent of the population was Muslim, and the majority of our family friends were Christian. Despite this, my parents maintained friendships across religious lines, but the strain of the war tested even the strongest of bonds. The tension outside our home was a constant reminder that, while we sought to rise above the divisions, the world around us wasn't always so forgiving.

As a little kid, I remember my father owning his own business, going from being very wealthy to losing everything he had built. As the war continued, the embargo got stricter and stricter, wiping out the supply chain where we could not even have access to basic needs for survival. It had become so bad that there were times that we didn't even have food in the fridge for weeks. My grandmother would bring things from her garden to help but this was limited as she still had her own large household to feed. This was a very hard time for most of the country. Imagine how difficult it was for my parents to feed five children.

Because of the hardships we faced, I had no choice but to start hustling at the age of twelve to help my parents make ends meet. There was no room for a typical childhood; survival took precedence. Whatever needed to be done, we did without hesitation.

We began by selling on the black market gasoline that was smuggled from Albania. It was a risky venture, fraught with danger. If caught, the authorities would confiscate everything, leaving us with nothing. We had to be extremely cautious, always watching our backs, and taking every precaution to avoid detection. The country was so poor and corrupt that the police would often seize the gas for themselves, using it to fill their own cars or selling it to make extra cash on the side. The line between law and crime blurred in those days, and we were caught in the middle, doing what we had to do to survive.

When I was fifteen years old, I remember being in the car with my mother when all of a sudden we saw a police checkpoint ahead. My thoughts went immediately to the gas canisters that we had hidden in the back seat covered with blankets. There was nowhere to turn to avoid the checkpoint. We had to attempt to pass through it. I was terrified. It wasn't just about getting into trouble; it was knowing that every single thing that was keeping our heads above water was there in the back of our car and it was going to be taken away. That feeling of hopelessness was so profound I can feel it in my bones even as I write these words. There was no way we could escape what was coming. We were in big trouble. These canisters were the difference between our family eating or not. As we slowed coming up to the checkpoint, I recognized the face of one of the police officers. It was an old neighbor of ours. I started to think that just maybe there was a glimmer of hope. Doubt and fear still battled within me, though. I didn't know him well and wasn't sure he would recognize me and even if he did, if he would have sympathy for our situation. We were not diehard criminals, just a family trying to make ends meet in the middle of a brutal war and the aftermath of it.

Sometimes the police tried to understand the desperation that the citizens were facing as they too were struggling. Sometimes you would get lucky and some of them would be agreeable to a bribe. I was not sure if this was one of those times. As the police officer came to our window, I gave him a smile with the hope that he would recognize me.

It made sense that they put up a random checkpoint here as on this particular road there were either only locals, which they did not have to worry about, or there were smugglers. At this particular moment we were the latter. The police officer looked at my mom, then at me, then back at my mom. With a straight face without a hint of recognition, he demanded our registration papers. His voice was deep and serious, showing no sign of friendliness. My heart sank, he didn't recognize us. He looked at the papers, looked at my mom, looked back at the papers, looked at me, back at the papers, looked in the back of the car where we had blankets covering what we were carrying. Long moments passed and he looked at me again, and finally spoke, "You look familiar, do I know you?" I am trying to keep my composure, fighting the nauseous feeling, just trying to stay calm and not betray what we had hidden in the car. It was so blatantly obvious, though, with the piles and the blankets covering the entire back seat. I answered him by saying, "Yes sir, we were neighbors." He looked again at my mother, glanced one more time in the back, and with that stern face that only a police officer can deliver, looked back at my mom. Again my heart sank once I saw that face. We were done. All of our livelihood was going to be taken away. I had no idea what would happen to us then. Once again my family was not going to have enough to eat, not going to be able to survive. He looked at another officer standing to the side and looked back at us one final time and said to my mom to drive off and not let him see us again. We would survive another day.

My country endured many years under the weight of a global embargo, leaving store shelves empty and barren. Even if you had money, there was nothing to buy. The influx of refugees from Bosnia, fleeing with nothing of their own in search of safety in Montenegro, only worsened the situation, saturating an already small job market.

Then came the era of the "Green Economy." This was a time when the sale of alcohol and cigarettes took place right on the streets, transforming them into bustling markets. It was reminiscent of the Saturday markets in Canada, where people shop for fresh food—but in Montenegro, this was no leisurely weekend activity. It was grueling, relentless work, with people toiling for twelve hours or more every single day. For many, it was the only way to make a living, and sometimes, it was a way to make very good money.

But the government was unpredictable during this period, veering between tolerance and repression. They would allow the "Green Economy" to thrive for a while, then suddenly crack down, declaring it illegal without warning. In an instant, countless livelihoods were destroyed. People who had finally found a way to get by were forced to start over from scratch, often sinking into debt in a world where survival was already a daily struggle. Those were hard days, and for many, the constant threat of losing everything again was a heavy burden to bear.

Once again, we found ourselves risking everything we had just to survive. Every day we lived with the looming threat that the authorities could raid the place where we were "working," stripping us of our last means of livelihood. During this period, we had our share of close calls with the police—moments that didn't always turn out as fortunate as the day at the checkpoint. Each encounter was a gamble, with our entire future hanging in the balance.

Despite the setbacks and the constant fear, we kept fighting, kept surviving. It wasn't easy, but our resilience paid off. Against the odds, we were doing better than many others at the time. We had learned how to navigate the uncertainty, how to adapt to the ever-changing rules of survival in a place where nothing was guaranteed.

As the late nineties approached, the rumblings of yet another war began to fill the air. The people were restless, weary from years of hardship, with no work and no hope in sight. My family was sinking deeper into debt, borrowing wherever we could just to keep our heads above water. It felt like we were trapped in a downward spiral, with nothing working anymore. It was during this dark time that my parents made a life-changing decision: they realized that the only way to secure a better future for their children was to leave our country behind.

My parents didn't want us to be defined by our religious beliefs but by who we were as individuals. They sought to give us a chance at peace and prosperity, away from the divisions that marked our homeland. Both in their forties—my mom in her early forties and my dad in his late—they had five children to care for, no knowledge of the language, and the daunting task of uprooting our lives to start anew in a place they had never even visited. Yet, they faced this challenge with unwavering strength and dignity—the kind that isn't often seen.

I vividly remember the day we left Montenegro, not even knowing which country we would end up in. Everything was uncertain, the future a vast unknown. We sold our house for so little it felt like we were giving it away, and left the country with just one piece of luggage each. We were starting from scratch, leaving behind everything familiar in search of a better life.

Our first stop was Bosnia, where we stayed for just over a year, trying to find a way out—a road to a new beginning, a place where we could live without the fear of being judged for our beliefs. That first month in Bosnia, we explored every opportunity, trying to figure out our next steps. My dad's cousin urged us to apply for immigration to Canada. It was a daunting process, with most people waiting three years or more. But thanks to my dad's cousin, we were given priority.

We could have left within six months, but a setback with my dad's health records revealed a stain on his lung, raising concerns about tuberculosis. This added to our wait as he had to prove it wasn't tuberculosis. During this time, we lived in a small apartment in Sarajevo, as refugees. The money from the sale of our house in Montenegro was gone within six months, and my sister and I had to work tirelessly to support our parents and the rest of siblings. It was a challenging time, but we were determined to keep moving forward, holding on to the hope of a better life.

Finally, in March 2001, we arrived in Edmonton, Canada. The adjustment was anything but easy; everything was different—the culture, the climate, even the food. Yet, amid the challenges, I was filled with excitement at the prospect of new beginnings for my family and me.

In that first year, I met the man who would later become my first husband. We married soon after, and because neither of us could endure the harsh winters of Edmonton, we quickly moved to Vancouver. It was there that I gave birth to my son. Being a mom was something I had always dreamed of, and the experience of pregnancy and giving birth felt like a dream coming true. I was so happy to finally embrace the role I had always longed for.

Let's Not Sugarcoat It

Living in Vancouver brought me joy. I loved the city, but a business opportunity eventually took us to Kelowna a few years later. This was a particularly happy time for me. We bought our first home, managed several businesses, and I gave birth to my daughter shortly after moving to Kelowna. In those early years, I felt a profound sense of fulfillment with my little family. Everything seemed to be falling into place—or so I thought.

However, as time passed, I began to notice cracks in what I once thought was a perfect life. There's a certain mentality ingrained in many older generations from the Balkans, where it's expected that a man can do as he pleases—go out, drink, party—while the wife, especially after having children, is expected to stay home, cook, clean, and certainly not complain. But I did complain. I wanted more from life. While being a mother and caring for my family was my dream, I also wanted a husband who chose to spend time with his family, rather than living as though he were still single. Slowly, I began to realize that something was missing, and that realization gnawed at me, growing stronger with each passing day.

And then things started to change. My husband lost his painting business, and I had to close the bakery I had opened with my parents in Westbank. The collapse of the painting business hit us hard, and we eventually lost our house. The economic crash of 2008 was like a tidal wave, and with so much uncertainty, nobody was interested in painting their homes when they weren't even sure they would still own them the following year.

During those difficult times, it felt as though much of what was happening was beyond our control. But even in the face of such adversity, I chose to hold on to hope, to keep moving forward, and to start over once again. Unfortunately, my husband chose a different path. He didn't have the fight left in him; he gave up. But I fought hard for my family for many years, determined to find a way through. Eventually, though, I had to face the truth—I had done everything I could, and it was time to move on.

Coming from a traditional family background, I had to learn how to balance my beliefs with the new world we were living in. I wanted to ensure that my children felt they belonged, that they were rooted in who they were, despite the challenges we faced. I realized, too, that having them young meant that we were growing up together, my children and I. We were learning from each other as we embarked on this new path, trying to build a life in a world that was so different from the one I had known.

It wasn't easy, especially after leaving my marriage with two young kids and nothing but our clothing. With no education or backup plan, we started from scratch—just like when my family immigrated to Bosnia. Kelowna didn't have job opportunities at the time, but my mom worked at a retirement home and helped me get a part-time job there to start somewhere.

It was tough juggling everything alone, but I was determined to succeed. I worked tirelessly, educated myself, and seized every opportunity to prove my worth. The journey was challenging but rewarding. Along the way, I met remarkable individuals who supported me, whether it was picking up my children from school or my manager allowing me to leave early to be there for them. I found a supportive environment at work, which was a blessing as it allowed me to provide for my children while making a living.

Another move in my life took me to Edmonton. Kelowna had become too expensive for a single parent, and with my ex never there to help, I found myself struggling to get ahead. I decided that a new town and new opportunities were the best option. I worked hard against all odds and eventually climbed to a director position within the same company I worked with in Kelowna. Despite life's setbacks, there were many blessings—some visible, some invisible, some known at the time, and others that I would only come to appreciate as time passed.

As a young mother with a strong will to live a beautiful life, I was determined not to let it go to waste. Moving to Edmonton also brought a man into my life, although I wasn't looking for one. My focus had always been on being a mom and ensuring my financial independence. Because of my tumultuous childhood and the often rapid changes in our financial standing, I didn't want to depend on anyone but myself.

After being single for many years and experiencing little success with men, I built a fortress around my heart, adopting a tough, masculine persona that kept most people at a distance. Then came Mark. From the moment he entered my life, he was different. Determined and patient, Mark never let anything deter him, not even the walls I had so carefully constructed. He was unwavering in his support, willing to wait as long as it took for me to lower my defenses, even just a little.

Mark became my knight in shining armor, a man who patiently chipped away at the barriers I had built. With him, I discovered that unconditional love truly does exist. He showed me that love could be gentle, kind, and enduring—a love that waits, that understands, and that never gives up. In Mark, I found the romance I had longed for, a love story I never thought would be mine, some faith, and an amazing father to my children.

Returning to Kelowna after meeting Mark, where he also proposed to me, was a wave of nostalgia. It was a city that held echoes of my past, a place where I had once built a life with my ex-husband and now found myself beginning anew. With Mark by my side, we embarked on a fresh journey together, launching wine tours and shuttle services in the very city that had once been my home away from home. Before moving to Edmonton I lived in Kelowna for fifteen years, and now it felt like I was reconnecting with a familiar part of myself while also creating something entirely new.

The venture brought its own set of challenges, navigating the ups and downs of a new business. Adding to the complexity, my fiancé underwent four major surgeries within the first two years of our relationship, which brought its own stress and uncertainty. I faced my own health crisis with a severe bout of COVID that left me bedridden for six weeks, unsure of my recovery.

These trials, though daunting, became profound lessons in resilience and perseverance. Each obstacle reminded me that life, with all its unpredictability, demands strength and adaptability. As I navigated through the shadows of uncertainty, I discovered that the true measure of success isn't found in the absence of hardship but in the courage to confront it.

I forged my path with determination and an unyielding commitment to my dreams. I learned that no matter how dark the days or how steep the climb, there is always light ahead if I keep moving forward. My journey, marked by challenges and triumphs alike, became a testament to the power of self-belief—a belief that doesn't merely survive the storm but thrives because of it.

In the end, it wasn't just about surviving; it was about embracing life in all its messy, unpredictable glory. I learned to celebrate the small victories, find joy in simple moments, and cherish the love and support that surrounded me, even when it was just my own strength I had to rely on.

Leaving my home country required immense courage and adaptability. Each new place and experience shaped my identity, teaching me the importance of flexibility, resilience, and faith. I learned to appreciate different cultures and perspectives, enriching my worldview and enhancing my personal growth. These experiences made me more open-minded and empathetic—traits that have been invaluable in both my personal and professional life. They gave me a different perspective on every person who leaves their home to seek a better tomorrow, seeing them as brave and strong souls with so much fight in them.

When I look to the future, I do so with the confidence that I can face whatever comes my way. I've built a life not on the foundation of what I've lost but on the strength of what I've gained—resilience, wisdom, and an unwavering sense of self. With that, I know that no matter what challenges lie ahead, I'll meet them with the same determination, faith, and love that has carried me this far.

As I move forward, I carry with me the lessons of my past, not as burdens, but as beacons guiding my way. My story is not just my own; it's a testament to the power of resilience and the enduring strength of the human spirit. I hope that in sharing my journey, I can inspire others to find their own courage, to embrace their own challenges, and to believe that no matter where life takes them, they have the power to shape their destiny. The future is uncertain, but with the wisdom I've gained and the love that surrounds me, I know that I am ready for whatever comes next.

SANELA SEHOVAC

Sanela Sehovac is a vibrant soul who believes in living life with passion, grace, and an unyielding spirit. Engaged to her knight in shining armor, Mark, and a proud mother to Gligor and Eva, Sanela's life is rich with love and purpose. Born and raised in Montenegro, she carries with her the tenacity and warmth of her homeland, qualities that have shaped her journey since moving to Canada in 2001.

Her love for the Okanagan and its exquisite wines inspired her to take the leap and start her own business. Today, Carpe Diem Tours is not just a service; it's a celebration of the region's finest offerings, shared with guests in both English and French, thanks to her innovative partnership with the local French Cultural Community.

Whether it's through her professional endeavors or her volunteer work, Sanela's goal is always the same: to make a difference in the lives of others.

The Okanagan Valley holds a special place in her heart, not just for its stunning landscapes and world-class wines, but for the community that welcomed her with open arms. No matter what challenges come her way, Sanela faces them with the grace of a loving mother, the strength of a passionate Montenegrin, and the heart of someone who believes in giving back. You can find Sanela on Instagram @montenegrina81 or @carpediemtourskelowna.

There comes a time when even the most loyal person must think about self-preservation.

CHAPTER 3

This Too Shall Pass

Crystelle Gordon

This too shall pass. A mantra repeated to myself daily for a time, a challenging time, arguably the most difficult period of my life thus far. I am not an addict, I never have been nor will I most likely ever be, but I loved one deeply for a time, almost 17 years.

I'll always remember the first time I laid eyes on him. The visceral reaction was like nothing I'd ever experienced, one of those world-stops-spinning, mind, body, and soul connection that was as intoxicating as it was thrilling. He came crashing into my life for a reason and for a season, with an intensity that left me breathless; and with him there would be no half measures, ever. Everything was to the extreme and I knew almost immediately, we were meant to be together.

I truly believe there is balance in all things—blame the Libra in me, or perhaps it is the Newtonian side of my science-minded brain. I believe that even though a moment can feel blissful, bright, and beautiful, somewhere at some point there is going to be a difficult period that can feel heavy, dark, and scary. The same can be said of certain people incessantly balancing between two places within themselves at one time, teetering on the brink of good and bad, kind and cruel, forever experiencing an ebb and flow from light to dark. Looking back now, I believe that is what I saw in the man that would become my husband.

Although never perfect, our relationship was good in the beginning. In that place of balancing the positive and the negative, the light with the dark, I was happy and content with where the proverbial scale sat. The positive outweighed the negative, and things were okay. Together we accomplished incredible things, we learned and grew together. Apart from myself, he was one of the hardest working people I had ever met and always striving for more, never lazy, always on the go, from one project to another. He was exceptional at sales and knew how to connect with most people incredibly quickly, knowing exactly what they needed to hear. As a wordsmith, he could tell stories in a way that captivated even the least enthusiastic members of a crowd, making them chuckle and even discretely smile.

He inspired me. I learned a great deal from just watching him, this charismatic man who could literally walk into a room and light it up. We both grew our individual empires and thrived, side-by-side, in our respective work environments, setting career goals, pushing each other to achieve them, only to set more, loftier ones.

We didn't limit ourselves to career aspirations but also worked tirelessly towards property goals. We purchased our first townhouse and taught ourselves how to be weekend-renovating-warriors, watching all the DIY YouTube videos available at the time. We would buy, renovate, and sell, then rinse and repeat. By the time we sold our last property together, we could both demolish and rebuild just about anything, having done our own plumbing, electrical, framing, mudding, tiling, and all other skills necessary to transform the average house into a pretty amazing home.

It was far from glamorous, weekend after weekend, hour upon hour spent covered in drywall mud and sawdust, sitting on a plywood floor with take-out pizza in the middle of what would someday be a great kitchen, looking at our handiwork. The exhaustion was so worth it, the literal blood, sweat, and tears put into everything we built, always together. We worked hard, tackling issues and setbacks, always together.

We taught each other that we could do whatever it was we wanted. We learned how to knock down walls and put them back up, figuratively as well as literally, and I am forever grateful for these skills.

It was also with this man that I became a mother, and what an amazing journey that has been. I will never forget holding our daughter for the first time, after a long and arduous delivery during which he never left my side. I also remember the pride and happiness in him at the birth of our first child, and how much love he immediately had for this little girl. It was a beautiful moment to share with someone you love.

He was brilliant, daring, and full of ideas, which I encouraged and supported. He started his own surgical import company which took guts, determination, and so much grit. I used to remind him that very few people had the mental fortitude to venture into the world he had, and he was crushing it. I originally kept my job to financially support our family as he got his company off the ground, but eventually joined him, and for a while it was amazing.

I think myself far from stupid but can acknowledge now just how very naïve I was all those years ago. Right from the beginning I turned a blind eye to how much he truly drank. Lies I told myself often sounded like this:

It wasn't that much.
He only drank in the evenings.
Sure he drank every evening, but he could always function the next day.
He had worked hard all day and needed that gin to unwind.
He had to entertain a lot for work and everyone else was always drinking at the various events.

These were all reasons I once believed and repeated to myself, excuses I gave to those around me who deigned to notice his habitual drinking.

I've now come to see and accept that he was a very high-functioning alcoholic. Until he wasn't. The high-functioning side of his habit started to erode. Slowly at first. So slowly that all my recent dissecting has been unable to pinpoint exactly when things changed, when the pivot happened, what the insipid catalyst was, or why I failed to see it coming. I will likely never have answers to those questions, and so many more.

The fact remains that he changed. It wasn't until one typical weekend morning that I realized just how much trouble we were in when I inadvertently grabbed his coffee mug at eight in the morning only to realize it was straight gin.

My once charming man began to prioritize other things. By the time our second daughter came along he was a very different person, a very different father. He no longer had patience. He still loved her, and us, but the devotion to his family had lessened. Sharp contrasts in my bank of maternal memories arise when I remember teaching our girls how to ride their bikes. With our first, he was so devoted, running behind her, cheering her on while I was on the sideline with a camera, grinning ear-to-ear, hooting and hollering my encouragement. With our second daughter, I was doing the running, the cheering, the grinning, hooting and hollering, while he sat at a distance, watching, criticizing, then chastising when she did fall over. He was usually about twenty ounces in by that point in the day.

Somewhere along the way, that proverbial scale had tipped. The darker side was getting heavier. His days were spent in a stupor. His nights as well. Mine were spent sleeping very little and lightly, listening and fearing what he might be up to. I spoke to counselors, I read books, I walked on eggshells not to say or do the wrong thing and kept our girls quiet around him.

Finally, I hired an interventionist who flew out from Toronto during COVID for his 186th intervention, boasting of a ninety percent success rate. I'd found an addiction treatment facility that was holding a spot open for us the day the interventionist came into our home. The facility was specialized in male patients, predominantly high achieving corporate-world males. The cost was exorbitant, but I had previously spoken to our mortgage broker and was going to refinance our home to get him into the treatment center. The days and nights leading up to the intervention were excruciatingly difficult. The outbursts were more frequent and more aggressive. He even hid my laptop one day, then my phone, thinking he was making me powerless and leaving me without means of communicating with the outside world. Thankfully, our then thirteen year old still had her phone so I was able to track my phone. It was June and he had hidden it in the pocket of a stored winter coat in our downstairs closet. He was toying with me and needed to feel like he had the upper hand. I kept trying to not upset the proverbial apple cart, knowing that the intervention was days away and I had so much hope. Hope that he would listen. Hope that some sort of awareness would hit him and he would realize what he was doing to himself, to us, and how he was destroying everything we had both worked so hard to build.

Unfortunately, two minutes were all it took for me to realize the intervention was going to fail. He began talking circles around the interventionist, skillfully turning the questions back on him. Ten minutes later he stormed out in an absolute rage. I was crestfallen.

Looking back, my biggest mistake was thinking I could influence him, guide him in this as we had done for each other so many times before. I've since learned better. For an addict to make a change they absolutely must choose it for themselves.

He lied a lot. He lied to me, but also to himself. He didn't think he had a problem, and most definitely not one that necessitated an intervention. He was furious at me, as well as with his brother who had been able to join us.

That being said, I didn't know how to give up, I was never raised to do so. I forgave, over and over, made excuses and even worse, believed them. I wanted to see the good, to see once again the man he had been years before, my man. I desperately wanted to find him again.

However there comes a time when even the most loyal person must think about self-preservation. The person I loved now thrived on causing exponentially more harm and hurt than good. I had reached the point where I was tired of being the only person trying to fix things. He was not mine to fix, not mine to save.

The day the intervention failed, I packed my bags and those of my two girls and left, which was by far one of the most difficult things I have ever had to do. The man I had so loved and cherished, had sadly become someone I could only tolerate yet still desperately wanted to help.

He had always been very eloquent and had become a master manipulator, skilled at convincing me and others that our reactions to his actions were the problem. We were being overly dramatic. At the time, through his various rants and monologues I was routinely left questioning my own sanity.

Was it maybe all my fault?

Did I lead him to drink?

Was I putting our family through this separation unnecessarily?

Was I wired wrong and simply unable to understand what he needed?

The doubt he succeeded in planting in me was strong. I was in my head questioning everything— all my thoughts, decisions, and actions were put in doubt. I was still holding on so tightly, thinking I had to, for the sake of our family and all our shared history. I was holding on to the hope that he would change and come back to us, back to our family, so we could once again be whole.

There was still a part of me that insisted on helping him, even though he refused all help from me and those around him. I continued to try to help him because he wouldn't help himself for the sake of me, our girls, or our family. The addiction had him completely turned. Every interaction was aggressive, every phone call became an attack on me, to the point where I had to start recording every conversation, which infuriated him even further. I had little choice as he would fabricate vicious claims about what had previously been said in an attempt to get me worked up. He wanted me to play along and be a pawn in his game of manipulation and control, to live in his intoxicated world and not leave him alone in it.

There were many times I wondered how we would all get through it, how it would end. I'd repeat to myself, this too shall pass. Deep down I knew it had to eventually end. We could not continue on like this forever—me caring for the girls alone, driving them over to see him when he seemed sober enough, recording conversations to make sure he would not be able to fabricate and twist things. I clung to the idea that we would get through it, wishing I could manifest a fast forward button to get to the other side of this horrible time in all our lives. This too shall pass.

I remember the day I reached the point where I was done. He had hurt me too much, put me through too many sleepless nights, I was completely drained and none of it could ever be taken back. For the sake of our girls, I wanted him to get help, to find himself again and be there for his daughters, be the father all little girls need to grow into young women who have healthy relationships with the opposite sex, but he and I were done.

I'd gone through every possible scenario in my head and was ready for just about anything, a real Girl Scout. I also knew that no matter what, my girls would be okay, because I had this. The unknown scared me, even terrified me at times, but I had to keep moving forward, for them, as well as for myself.

It felt like an eternity of constantly walking on eggshells, never sure what mood he would be in and how intoxicated he would get every day, and then, two years after the failed intervention and the girls and I having left, a loud knock came at my door in the middle of the night. Two police officers came into my house to tell me he had passed away. I collapsed. All I kept asking myself over and over again was what will I tell the girls. I was in shock. Then a wave of resentment hit me. Such resentment and anger at how he had thrown away and wasted such a beautiful life on the bottle.

I was grateful that I stayed by his side as long as I did. I was grateful that I did all that I could. I don't feel guilty for the loss of his life, it was his choice to make, as was the decision to consume every single drink. I know we tried. We all tried to get through to him and what causes me the most sadness is that by the end there were no figurative mirrors in his world, only myths and fabrications of his mind. He never truly saw what he had become.

I did not unlove him overnight. I could never. I unloved him slowly, one painful piece at a time. Painful because together, with that freaking blue bottle of gin, he broke my heart. I've since grown a new heart, one much stronger, yet still kind, caring, and full of love to give. That too has been a process, a beautiful one, and taken time.

I firmly believe that the Universe only dishes out what we can take. I didn't always feel that way, this particular nugget of wisdom also took time to sink in. It was difficult to believe, especially while I was smack dab in the middle of what felt utterly unsurmountable. However, trusting that I could handle whatever was happening did help me, and repeating to myself that this too shall pass, gave me some comfort and I leaned into it. I also believe a part of me needed to experience the darkness in order to better appreciate the light, now and for the rest of my life. I am fortunate that I had my girls to remind me of that every day. Though unconsciously done by them, they pushed me to move forward and keep telling myself we would be okay. We had to be. It was a choice then and it still is now. I try to be the best parent possible, to guide them, nurture them, love and support them. I try to show up every single day.

Another lesson I learned is that no matter how small or great my hurt felt, I couldn't rush my healing. I couldn't push it away, sweep it under the so familiar proverbial rug, or drown it out with distractions, no matter how much I wanted to. There was no fast forward button. I had to feel it, sit with it, be with myself. My experience taught me that if your healing step is thoroughly felt, at your own pace, you have a better chance of truly liking the person that comes out of it in the end. I also learned that I didn't have to fight for closure or seek explanations and answers. I couldn't. I also didn't have to justify how I was processing my pain to anyone but myself. I trusted that my healing would end once it was time for me to step into something greater and I wasn't going to fight that journey.

There were times my human instinct had me wishing I could go back in time and do things differently, somehow change the outcome so the really horrible things, the ones that had me curled on the foot of my bed wracked by sobs, wouldn't hurt quite so much. But I know now that I don't want to change a thing. I am who I am today, and where I am because I deeply loved an alcoholic. I take comfort in the fact that all the heartache and self-doubt I went through is partially responsible for the happiness I feel and the love I have in my life today. I am indeed very fortunate to have in my world the most amazing people. People who make everyday brighter, easier, calmer, and do so without being asked. People who know my soul. Life has a funny way of bringing us exactly who, what, where we need, at the exact moment we need them.

I am so much stronger now, and so grateful for all that I have. Today I get to enjoy many amazing moments. I get to revel in the fact that a great storm has passed, one through which I have learned so much about myself and what I am truly capable of, one I survived. I have learned to set boundaries, for my own protection, as well as for my personal growth and that of those I love and cherish.

When I look back at this whole journey, I want people to know and recognize how slippery the slope is. Do not have blinders on. Countless people's lives are touched by alcohol and alcoholism, whether personally navigating those tumultuous waters themselves or through a loved one suffering from this illness. It is an ugly addiction, hidden in plain sight, that has the potential to latch onto a person's soul, taking over their life until even those around them, often those who likely partook in consumption with them, or those who love them most, can no longer recognize them. Over time, if you don't really look at what is actually going on, little by little, drink by drink, a wonderful person gets lost. I don't wish that for anyone, or anyone's loved one. Also remember that all we have is the power to keep moving forward, and when things get really bad, remind ourselves that *this too shall pass.*

CRYSTELLE GORDON

As a single mom and entrepreneur in Kelowna, Crystelle Gordon juggles life as best she can...while walking the proverbial tightrope! Mother to two amazing girls, director of a surgical import company and owner/operator of the new-to-Kelowna Body Bar Laser Clinic, Crystelle absolutely loves talking about skin, anti-aging, and how to help men and women age as gracefully as possible. In addition to a laser clinic, Crystelle is also soon opening the Kelowna campus of Body Bar Laser Academy to train and certify others who share her passion for lasers. There may not be a Holy Grail of eternal youth but there most definitely is a lot we can do today with technology to look as good as possible, at any age :) Connect with Crystelle at @crystelle2021 or @bodybarkelowna.

What a gift it is to show up for myself and receive the healing energies and wisdom of connecting with nature.

CHAPTER 4

Fueling the Fire Within: Embracing the Marathon of Life

Shannan Roberts

There's nothing quite like the feeling I get from tying my running shoe laces and hitting the trails. As I hit my stride, I feel the ground beneath my feet and my breathing falls into a rhythm. The air on my face and the solitude of the forest invigorates me, and my heightened sense of smell brings me peace. Running allows my brain to slow down and provides a therapeutic pause to unravel my brewing emotions and reflect. Some days, solutions to life's challenges become more clear, and empower me to make better decisions. Despite tiredness and burning legs, I'm exhilarated as I become one with the trail. It's in those moments that I realize that running and being in nature is essential for my physical and mental well-being.

Running not only keeps me mentally and physically well, it has changed my life. In April 2003, amidst the breathtaking landscapes of Yellowknife, Northwest Territories, I made the decision to commit to a personal goal of completing my first full marathon. Little did I know this decision would not only challenge me physically but also touch my heart in ways I never imagined.

A few months earlier, at twenty-four years old, I'd met a woman at a conference who completed a full marathon with the Arthritis Society's *Joints In Motion* (JIM) program. I couldn't help but be curious to learn more about what it was like to run a full marathon. At that point in my life, I liked to jog occasionally, mainly on my own as an outlet to be physically active and release stress, but I'd never done anything so structured or formal.

Not long after that conference, I made a commitment to train for my first marathon with the Joints In Motion program in Canada. When you sign up to JIM you get assigned to a location based on the timing of training and race dates. I was so happy to find out I'd be running in Honolulu, Hawaii and that my dear friend Kirsten would be joining me. Registering meant we had to commit to raise $6,000 for the Arthritis Society's Edmonton chapter. For us, the idea of giving back to a meaningful cause and raising more awareness ignited our sense of purpose.

The initial challenges of training for Honolulu were overwhelming. Not only did we lack experience, but we'd never raised that much money before. Both the extensive prep and perseverance required to fundraise that amount transformed my perspective, and set me on a remarkable path of personal growth. The way I see it, raising the funds and my commitment to training and crossing that particular finish line mirrors the many complexities of my life.

Like all of us, I experienced many setbacks, doubts, fears, and insecurities that surfaced along the way and paralleled the emotional hurdles I was facing in pursuit of my goals. For example, when I first set out for my goal I didn't count on the number of times I wouldn't feel like I had the energy for training, or the number of times that fear would creep in and I'd doubt whether I had the physical and mental strength to push on. Inevitably, I also had a few small injuries, and even got sick with the flu at the tail end of training. The flu virus attacked my lower back, and I couldn't move without extreme pain which was really scary. On top of the fear, I was told only weeks before the marathon that I couldn't train for a minimum of ten days. Still, I persevered, unable to stop thinking about the commitment I'd made to myself, and my goal to support the Arthritis Society.

Despite the many challenges training brought, it was also really exciting. Everything was new, from learning about recommended running clothes, supplements, and accessories to the latest in running shoe technology. Similarly, learning about nutrition and which foods made me feel energized and healthy was also a period of trial and error. I learned to wear an exercise belt to carry gel packs, energy cubes, and ibuprofen for long runs over twenty-five kilometers just in case. I am very grateful that running has taught me the power of connecting with nature. My training was mainly outdoors, and this anchored in my lived experience that spending time outdoors enabled me to find inner peace, be more grounded, cherish the beauty and wisdom of mother nature.

As our training progressed, the days quickly turned into weeks and months; until it was finally time to board our flight for the race. We left Yellowknife a few days early in order to acclimatize. Once we landed, the Edmonton Joints In Motion coaches and community greeted us and we were given the most fragrant and beautiful leis upon arrival to begin our first Hawaiian adventure.

On race day, there was so much energy on the marathon grounds, the music was pumping, the good vibes flowing, and supporters with signs stretched in the distance as far as the eye could see. For me, the best part of the race was the home stretch when I descended from Diamond Head Crater along a downhill stretch enjoying the warm sun, ocean breeze and the race entertainment crew blasted *Chariots of Fire* for extra inspiration as we crossed the finish line. What a thrill it was to accept my first medal, and join the masses of limping runners; experiencing the inability to walk downstairs normally for at least two days.

Post race I felt elated and empowered. We arrived home from Hawaii with a renewed sense of pride—our finisher medals were symbols of the highs and lows our training had brought us. For us, the experience wasn't just about crossing a finish line. It was about touching hearts and embodying the true spirit of the JIM slogan, *Train, Travel, Triumph*. The stories of courage and resilience from those battling arthritis, and the support from friends and family fueled my desire to continue running. Through my marathon experiences I have come to realize that nature is not simply a backdrop for adventures, but a sacred space that nurtures my mind, body and soul.

Riding the high of the pride from our recent achievement, within a month of arriving home my friend and I began delivering our "Get Your Groove On!" healthy lifestyle workshops to young women. It was an idea born during a low point in our training when we didn't think we were on track to raise our $6000 goal. In a last ditch effort, we decided to meet at our favorite local coffee shop to brainstorm all the ideas we could think of to raise funds. It's there that we channeled our creativity and organized an educational workshop for youth focusing on what we learned. We settled on four main teaching points, the importance of personal power and self-esteem, fitness, nutrition, and goal setting. We titled the workshop, "Get Your Groove On!" We submitted the proposed workshop to Sport North Federation in hopes of receiving the remaining funds needed to reach our fundraising goal. Our workshop was very well received and through this we reached our goal of $6000 and created a workshop that felt near and dear to our hearts and were proud to share.

On top of that, the workshop created a huge buzz and was in high demand across communities in the Northwest Territories. After a couple of years it was time to evolve it into something more sustainable, a summer camp program called Taiga Adventure Camp (TAC). TAC provided a leadership camp experience for youth ages 11-18 across the territory. Today, after a number of strategic partnerships and connections with the youth, the program continues to thrive and Taiga Adventure Camp is now the Northern Youth Leadership. Being the co-founder of Northern Youth Leadership with my friend is definitely the contribution and legacy that I'm most proud of in my life.

Over the years, running has become my preferred way to connect with the world around me, and continues to relieve stress and enhance my overall wellbeing. Since Honolulu I've run in a number of marathons. Running marathons in different parts of the world has opened my eyes to the diverse beauty of our planet, from the lush boreal forests in Canada, to awe-inspiring mountain terrain, desert landscapes, and ocean routes inviting me to experience the flow of life, and splendor of nature's elements in all its forms.

In 2004, I decided to register for the Yellowknife Marathon where my love of running quickly transformed from something I did, to a huge part of my identity. Because of this, it was a sport I wanted to share with others in my community, so I decided to become a nationally certified running coach.

In 2005, I made the commitment to train for and run another marathon. I decided I wanted to experience running in new and exciting places in the world. My love for running and globetrotting is still a passion twenty years later. It's been a fascinating way to experience new landscapes, trails, and cities while making connections with new friends from all corners of the world. It's my pathway to a state of flow where my worries dissipate, and I feel a deep sense of connectedness with myself, my surroundings, and nature. As a result, encouraging others to explore their passions and set stretch and ambitious goals has become a central theme in my life. I discovered that my purpose is to help others to seek experiences and uncover their strengths to foster personal growth.

My purpose and deeper "why" to serve others has become my

guiding force, and supported me through hard moments of doubt, pain, and uncertainty. Each stride, each trail, and each run acts as a gateway to release the burdens that weigh on me. And, each marathon has offered me a new perspective and deeper appreciation of life.

Starting in 2005, when I was visiting family in Northern Ontario and planned to run the Toronto Marathon. This was a very special run for me because my mom joined me and walked her first half marathon to celebrate over a decade since she had successfully quit smoking. I will never forget one of the musicians on the sidelines who was singing, "You Can't Always Get What You Want," which at the time felt like a far cry from the *Chariots of Fire* vibes in Honolulu. Initially the song's title seemed like a statement of defeat, but upon reflection I realized that it carries a beautiful and profound message about acceptance, resilience, and understanding the face of life's uncertainties and disappointments. It reminded me that life is full of twists and turns, and the ability to adapt, learn, and find joy in the present moment is what builds our character.

In March 2011 I ran the Labor of Love Marathon which is close to Las Vegas, Nevada. The marathon runs along the paved Lovell Canyon Road, and the high altitudes across rocky terrain was new for me and extreme. The marathon start time was seven a.m., creating an extreme swing in temperatures from near freezing at the race start to extremely hot by the time I finished. At this particular race, I made the mistake of trying a new sport drink, and I ended up violently throwing up on the side of the path. I learned there is a time and place for experimentation and mid-way through a marathon isn't either of those. And this may be the only time in my life I will have the opportunity to boast a first place finish for my gender and age category. I was over the moon thrilled, and happy to bring home a small cactus plant, and of course my finisher medal.

In September 2019 I ran the Cape Town, South Africa Sanlam Marathon. This is a global city race and is open to a whole spectrum of running enthusiasts, including a large number of elite and wheelchair athletes who both start before the general group of social runners. This was my first race after a traumatic motor vehicle accident that resulted in a concussion, soft tissue damage, and several years of recovery. To prepare for this race I dedicated each kilometer to special people throughout my life. Early on, around the seven kilometer mark, one of my greatest fears happened. The race was very congested with people actually touching as we ran, and I didn't notice there was a speed bump under my feet. As I tripped, and fell to the ground, my arms moved forward to break my fall and my Apple Watch screen smashed. I scraped my knees and the palms of my hands. Blood ran down my legs, and bits of gravel were stuck in my hands, and for a moment I thought it might be time to quit. But, I walked and took a ten minute breather, then managed to continue running despite being shaken up and aching. When I think back, my strongest memories are my perseverance to push through, and the friendliness of South Africans in the Mother City who invited me to celebrate and take in the sights along Camps Bay.

Next was the Stockholm, Sweden Marathon in June 2022 with my colleague and dear friend, Amber. During this race I was reminded about the importance of keeping anything for race day in your carry-on luggage. Sadly her luggage, including everything she needed to race her first ever marathon, was lost. She needed new runners and proper clothing which was really inconvenient. Even though it's a road race in an urban setting, there were lush green spaces, parks, gardens, and an archipelago of islands. The tranquil waters, birds in flight, and picturesque historic buildings were stunning. The lesson that stands out for me for this marathon was the importance of training and preparation, including packing for race day.

Last but not least in May 2024, I ran the Oak Bay Victoria, Canada half-marathon as part of my training for the Willemstad, Curaçao Marathon later in the year. It was the first time I experienced road closures and severe traffic enroute to a race which added an element of stress, and resulted in me having to walk five kilometers before the race even started. Thankfully my friend Brian saved the day! He picked up my race packet, attached the bib to my shirt, and met me at the start line. I'm so grateful as this was my only chance to join close to the actual start time, starting just five minutes late. It was a chilly day with light rain, and I appreciated the volunteers and cheerful supporters. One sign I especially loved simply said "GO STRANGER GO!" People cheering were holding Mario mushroom powerup signs to hit, and friendly people offered high fives, shaking bells and noisemakers, and shouting words of encouragement. My highlight was definitely the massage I received from Brian of the West Coast College of Massage Therapy. It served as a great reminder of the healing benefits of massage and the importance of self-care.

For me, marathon races have been one of the greatest gifts of my life. Each marathon has offered me a unique experience and continues to shape my perspective and deepen my connection with my physical body, with nature, and the world around me. The lessons I've learned extend far beyond the world of running. As I reflect on the resilience of the human spirit, and the importance of commitment in life, the significance is that the marathon of life is not just about reaching the finish line but embracing the journey with self-love. Perseverance in the face of challenges has served me countless times in my career and personal life. It's so beautiful coming together to support a common cause. The principles of commitment and resilience have intertwined with my professional life and projects. As a business consultant and advisor I've leveraged these values to guide businesses in their pursuits.

In my mind, the power of setting ambitious goals and striving to achieve them can't be beat. The elation and gratitude I feel every time I cross the finish line has led me to a deeper appreciation for my body, my relationship with nature, my community, and the shared journey. Running continues to inspire me to explore diverse countries, landscapes and to immerse myself in different cultures. While running has been mainly a personal endeavor, it has also become a catalyst for empowering others.

What a gift it is to show up for myself and receive the healing energies and wisdom of connecting with nature. Whether it's the literal trail beneath my feet or the figurative journey of life, the act of commitment—releasing control, surrendering to my fears, enduring the challenges, and connecting deeply with myself carries a profound sense of fulfillment.

Running helps me to leave it all on the trail, whether it's the actual trail or a symbolic moment in life. I can be having the worst day, with the weight of the world on my shoulders from worries that are stressing me out, and it is as if the problems float away as soon as I start running. Every time I pound my foot into the dirt, a little bit of pressure, worry, or fear are released. The serenity of the trails and the rhythmic sound of my breathing are my companions on my transformative journey.

I encourage you to reflect on your own relationship with nature. My advice is to create your own personal practice and set aside time each week, even fifteen minutes can provide noticeable wellness benefits. Choose a sit spot in the woods along a trail, near a tree, in a park, or a garden to observe the beauty around you. I invite you to close your eyes and take a deep breath to fully immerse yourself in the present moment as you offer gratitude to the forest for its healing presence. Allow a sense of connection to wash over you as you meditate on the peacefulness and abundance of the natural world. Reflect on all five of your senses. Give thanks for the beauty that surrounds you, the healing energy that embraces you, and the wisdom that guides you. Let us carry this gratitude as we continue our marathon of life, fueled by the fire within and the love that nature so generously bestows upon us.

For me, running a marathon symbolizes the gift of devotion—to myself, my aspirations, and the path that lies ahead. In leaving it all on the trail, I embark on an odyssey, where self-discovery, communal bonds, and the splendor of nature converge to enrich and inspire our souls. I am most excited for what the future holds in my marathon of life, all the places running is going to take me next, the people I will meet, and the ways I will connect with myself and nature on a deeper level.

Running a marathon may not be for you, but what is it that fuels that fire within your soul?

SHANNAN ROBERTS

Shannan Roberts is a mother, entrepreneur, nature enthusiast, and conscious leader who dedicates herself to pursuing her many passions and enriching the lives of those around her. She is co-author of the Amazon bestsellers: bLU Talks, Volume 11 and Self-Love Elevated Volume 2.

Shannan has over 20 years of experience in business and economic development, working with purpose-driven organizations and diverse groups, including Indigenous communities across Canada and internationally. She is co-owner of Prep Academy Tutors of Interior BC, which strives to be the gold standard in private in-home, virtual tutoring and educational services. You can connect with me on LinkedIn at www.linkedin.com/in/shannanstella/ and on Instagram at @thejoyofhumanconnection.

Experiences are embedded with the full spectrum of emotions; this is life and what it means to be alive.

CHAPTER 5

Love. Live. And Learn.

Dr. Brett Phillips

The night my life was instantly shattered, I was lying in bed next to my wife when she rolled over, looked me straight in the eyes and announced that she didn't love me anymore. In that moment my heart was ripped out of my chest and my life changed forever.

The first time I saw my wife it was truly love at first sight for me. I was a senior in university and she was a freshman and I instantly felt a sensation emanating from my heart, which moved through my body from my head to my toes. Experiencing that complete body rush, I instantly knew she was going to be my one and only, my wife.

The year flew by when I completed my undergraduate degree. Thoughts of my original plan to travel overseas resurfaced—but I had fallen in love. I truly was in a dilemma, as I still had the desire to travel but at the same time I didn't want to lose my newfound love. After a lot of debating, coupled with meditation and consultation, I decided to pursue a four-year Naturopathic Medicine doctorate. This required a move to Vancouver. I specifically remember thinking that I'd ask her to join me and that we'd live together and perhaps we would even start a family.

The following week I asked her if she would like to move with me and she said yes but also stated that she was pregnant. Manifestation at its finest! Before long we made our move. We'd discussed and planned that we wanted to have a big family. While I was in medical school we had two children and then two children shortly after. During that time we had accumulated student loans and bank loans. Fortunately, we had some family support to ease the financial burden. Together we also arrived at the decision that a priority would be that my wife would stay at home with the kids and that I would be the income earner.

Even today I continue to be so grateful for that decision because we have the greatest four kids. Anyone that has met them has reported back to us how each child is so incredible. They're intelligent, well-spoken, speak their mind, and that they are kind, thoughtful, loving individuals. I truly believe having that stability of a stay-at-home parent has greatly contributed to each of them being such lovely humans.

So to hear the words, "I don't love you anymore," from the person I'd spent half my life in love with, shattered my very existence. I felt broken, and if I'm being truly honest, I haven't been whole since. As I am writing this, I'm still trying to figure it all out and put the pieces together in an effort to make sense of it all. At times I feel like I am just about to understand and make sense of it and then I realize that there's still so much more to understand.

Like in any marriage, we had some ups and downs, though we never really fought. We were opposites, yet like it has been said, opposites attract. I was the social butterfly while my wife preferred being at home. Many times after we'd put the kids to bed, I would head out on my own to hang out with friends and my wife would stay in. I was able to maintain the social life that I enjoyed and she got to stay home and be cozy like she preferred. This seemed to work for us both. I was always faithful, and came home at the end of a night out with my friends. For many years, we went on like this. We were happy and loving and we adored the life we had with our family of six.

Looking back, we both came into our relationship with our own experiences, histories, and traumas. In the midst of our relationship, some things that had not previously been dealt with appeared. And although I was trying my best to understand and be supportive, we probably didn't have an adequate strategy nor the support that was truly needed to resolve our issues together. The issues that were arising were serious and obviously we were in need of professional help. Over time, these unresolved issues and our individual pressures that we carried through the roles we had within the family unit started to weigh on our relationship.

I also was quite aware of the many hats I was required to wear. One responsibility was the weight that was on my shoulders of being the sole breadwinner in our family and ensuring that financial stability would be maintained. Each day I dealt with patients' mental, emotional, and/or physical illnesses which required my thoughtfulness and attentiveness but also drew on my emotional energy. The nature of my practice is such that many of my patients were in a state of chronic pain. Others were in their end stages of life, which can take a tremendous emotional toll on the caregiving physician.

Another responsibility was taking care of the business side of my practice. I was handling the marketing, networking, and financials which often required working some evenings. This created much internal conflict as I tried to be present as a dad and husband. I felt the immense weight that I was carrying on my shoulders. My ability to stay in the present moment and display a carefree demeanor and friendly smile often created the illusion that what I was doing was easy. But it rarely was.

Over the years, we started to drift further and further apart. I asked repeatedly for us to get professional help to try to save our family but my wife wasn't interested in exploring that option. I was so broken by this point. I easily remember crying myself to sleep many nights. The only thing that was holding me together was our children and my need to provide for them. Without my involvement and financial contribution I imagined them out in the street. By now it had become obvious to the children that our marriage had fallen apart. I was losing my light, my joy, and any purpose to my life. It was then I faced my darkest moment followed by a solution—an escape—that would allow me to not go through this heartache anymore.

Thank God for my children, my close friends, and my father, who have all been my solid ground through this. For well beyond a year my wife and I drifted even further apart. Things got so distant between us that she even suggested that I find someone outside of our marriage to meet my physical needs because they were no longer going to be met within our marriage. I was still very much in love with my wife and was focused on saving my marriage so I didn' take her up on her offer. As the months passed, my wife started spending more time outside our home and with new people. She was moving on with her life and it was breaking me.

I decided it was time to try to shift my state of mind and to see if I could create a life in spite of my soul feeling so broken. I had a few DMs that I'd been ignoring so I went ahead and finally responded. The next thing I knew, I had four Internet girlfriends and I felt a little bit of life that I had not felt in years return to my soul. Within a month I grew closer to one woman. We shared about our lives and realized that we were going through similar challenges. I felt that this was the first time in the past couple years that someone cared. I felt like I cared. It activated something inside of me. This woman lived out of town and as our conversation expanded, we grew closer. I thought there was a possible opportunity to meet someone with respectability, so I planned to go and meet her, all the while hoping that my wife would stop me when I told her everyday for a week that I was going out of town. This was my cry for validation, for a hope or glimmer that she still loved me. But she didn't, so I went.

In meeting this woman my light and my vitality turned back on. I was reminded that I am desirable. I had value. Somebody actually cared for me. Appreciated me. Laughed with me. Enjoyed my company. I was lovable. It inspired me. It woke me from my depression. Needless to say I was recharged. It was not the way I had wanted it. I wanted my wife, but still with all my efforts, she didn't want anything to do with me. So odd as it was, I was grateful that my wife had offered this hall pass that took me years to come to acknowledge and to utilize.

Unfortunately, I came home to find the place in absolute chaos and my wife and children missing. My bedroom had been ransacked and my online accounts had all been broken into. Even in my darkest moment I had remained faithful for years; only out of desperation and need to feel loved and desired did I make this trip to Vancouver. When I finally heard from my wife, the conversation was horrific and heartbreaking. It was the official end of our relationship. I felt like I'd been manipulated and set-up, made out to be the bad guy. I was devastated. I still have so many unanswered questions as to why it all fell apart.

Since then I have navigated through the start and end of other relationships. These experiences have allowed me to establish a foundation within myself, which has provided me with the understanding of the importance and necessity of going forward.

And I can say that after the heartbreak of my marriage ending I found it difficult to allow myself to fully feel because it would be too hard. There were so many things I needed to do and take care of, so many responsibilities like operating two medical clinics and helping hundreds of patients, as well as being a father to four. It was a lot to manage.

I had been just going and going for so long with my head down trying to make it all work. I did finally come to the realization that I was merely existing, feeling numb. I felt like I didn't have the capacity to go into the pain I was experiencing and it became clear that I had been avoiding it.

I have now started to see more and more of the red flags that until this time I had been unaware of.

I have learned that healing takes time and that it takes one's commitment to orchestrate change and to move forward. It is a commitment to yourself and I know that my process toward the healing of my heart started with me getting back into what I know is my foundation, which is a healthy body and mind. For me some of those things include a nutritional component, moving my body, being active, working out, and getting out into nature. I believe that when we take care of our physical body, then we are more open to shifting our mindset and then ultimately healing on that spiritual level. I have surrounded myself with those that I love most. I continue to immerse myself with my kids, with my dad, and with those friends who I know I can count on.

I started practicing gratitude every single morning instead of just going on my phone and scrolling social media or checking emails or looking at the news. Very often the gratitude is as simple as now having the ability to live in the light, enjoy life, and realize I am in control so I will not be dragged into those dark places again. And so often it is the simplest things for which one needs to be grateful. I have discovered that gratitude has a snowball effect and the more it is utilized the more you realize that there is a lot that you actually do care about in life, with that understanding you can embrace life, as there is just so much to live for.

It has taken me a long time to get to the point of being able to release negative emotions in an appropriate way. I am gradually healing as I let go of the methods that I had used to suppress my emotions, to hide my feelings, and to run away from the pain. As I started to release those thoughts and feelings, some of which had become habits and no longer served me, I began to wake up to new feelings and tap into those former healthy ones that did serve a purpose. Along with my restoration, an abundance of energy has surfaced, which has also reassured me that I am headed in the right direction.

To reiterate that for some, like myself, it will be necessary to hit bottom and to go to those depths of experiencing heartbreak, grief, anger, and resentment. It is a reminder that our experiences are embedded with the full spectrum of emotions; this is life and what it means to be alive.

And so this has been my journey so far, with my heart that had been totally broken and continuing to heal. With establishing new relationships, I continue to learn more about myself and the world around me which has taught me to pay attention to and respect my morals, my values, and my boundaries.

I am grateful for all the lessons along the way because I know that I am evolving into the person I am meant to be. I am optimistic that I will be able to experience a full range of natural, healthy emotions, be in a place of peace, and to be able to not only give love but now be receptive to opening my heart to receiving love.

DR BRETT PHILLIPS

Dr. Brett Phillips is a Naturopathic physician who has been in private practice for the past 17 years. He lives in Kelowna BC with his four children Maximus, Theodore, Athena, and Atticus. His Naturopathic practice is a holistic approach of mind, body, and spirit medicine. He believes your quality of life is a product of who you hang out with and your daily habits. He teaches the foundations of healthy diet, daily exercise, living mindfully, and getting restful sleep using various biohacks, such as IV therapies, regenerative injections, therapies, supplements and herbal medicines, traditional Chinese medicine, and acupuncture, as well as Naturopathic adjustment. He embodies these practices, as he believes leading by example for his family, his patients, and his community. He enjoys spending his spare time skiing with his family and summers on his motorcycle. Connect with Brett at info@naturopathichealthcare.ca or www.naturopathichealthcare.ca.

It's okay that you were done being that girl who just rolled up her sleeves and carried on.

CHAPTER 6

A Love Letter in Grief: A widow's journey of strength and resilience

Chantaal Doucet

If I could go back in time and send you a letter on the night you tried to drown yourself in the tub while your husband's ashes sat beside you, I'd tell you that it took trying to regurgitate the memories of your life on paper to make me realize just how much you'd been through.

From abandonment, abusive relationships, a teen pregnancy, facing death, to extreme trauma and assault, you've faced some of the greatest losses any human could face. And one day, you'll look back to that day you sat fully clothed in that tub as the water got cold and you finished a second bottle of wine, and think, "How could one human endure so much pain in one lifetime?"

Because, you truly have. Looking back now, I can see where it all started. Where all those seeds for your future feelings of abandonment and loneliness were planted. You didn't really stand a chance from day one. What do you think your little baby mind was thinking when your teen mom wrapped you in a little blanket, wrote a note and left you on your father's doorstep? And even though you now understand that was what she truly thought was best for you, it didn't change the abandonment your tiny body felt as a result.

And then, when you were only a little girl, your father left the very night of your eighth birthday. Remember how you clung to him tightly. To this day, the smell of whiskey and cigarettes still reminds you of that night. That's the night your life changed and you realized the first eight years of your life had been a lie. That your mother wasn't your mother. Suddenly now, it makes sense why you never felt like you belonged, why it always felt like she liked your sister, her birth child, best. Looking back I can see this wounding of being left, being abandoned, not being chosen, and how it led you to constantly seek to belong.

I'd tell you that the feeling of never belonging is a hard feeling to bear. I'd remind you that we all carry wounds and traumas from our childhood, walking around with this little inner child inside of us that is screaming for attention, that is wishing that they could have what they desired from that place long ago just to be seen, to be heard, to be held, to be loved.

You'll think of that day in the bathtub with the bottles of wine and you'll think of that little girl screaming to be loved. The one who was ripped from the only home she knew and put back in her birth mother's home only to suffer further abuse and chaos and more evidence for the belief that she didn't belong.

You'll think of all those moments you were so strong, where you fought back. Including the moment years later where you drove for an hour after your boyfriend tried to kill you and you'll remember that we all have a breaking point. You'll remember all the things you endured and how on the night in that tub it felt like all of the pillars of the foundation you'd built to protect that inner child within you were ripped from underneath you.

Do you remember how you held your knees tightly to your chest feeling the static in your mind building and the boiling of your skin, but how cold the tile floor was, and the way you were literally soaking the floor with tears? You could feel the stickiness of the tears on your cheeks, which made you crawl into the bathtub drawing the water while asking your thirteen year old daughter to bring you a bottle of wine. I want you to know I forgive you for not being able to wear that heavy mask of being strong for a moment longer. It's okay that you'd finally had enough and chose to lay in that tub fully clothed, the water freezing, consuming two bottles of wine and shedding your weight in tears.

Do you remember how you thought you'd never leave that tub? And how for the first time in forty-two years, you wanted to give up? How you shamed yourself for no longer wanting to be strong. How you thought for the first time ever, "What if I could just take my life?" I'd tell you that night an essence of the woman you once were was no more.

I know you left fragments of your soul in that tub that night. You left the wife you were only two years prior—to the day to be exact, the mom, the friend, the woman you were. The one you were until the moment your husband took his life and killed your light, and stole the color from your children's eyes. It's okay that two years later in that tub you felt so unworthy and angry for having to carry the blame he placed on you for ending his life. It's okay that you felt sad. It's okay that even though you loved him, in that tub you remembered the parts of him that made you angry. The moments where he lost control, moments where he wasn't fully in his right mind, moments where his own trauma took over and the triggers were so loud.

It's okay that you felt angry at the way you saw him spiraling and didn't understand it. Didn't understand depression and anxiety because you'd always been the person who just keeps on going, stopping was never a thought; never an option for you. It's okay that in that tub that night you were done being that girl who just rolled up her sleeves and carried on. I forgive you for not wanting to look for a way to turn something negative into a positive. It's okay that you were mad and that you couldn't find compassion in that moment and instead felt anger towards the man you once looked up to for your shelter, for your protection. The man you once thought of as your rock. And it's okay that you felt resentful to the way he often crumbled and gave in to these spirals of depression and anxiety, as if they would overwhelm him. It's okay that you felt obligated to push him and frustrated at the many times you'd begged him just to choose differently.

You are not responsible for his actions, but it's okay that you sat in that tub and blamed yourself for telling him he'd be better off without you. And it's okay that in that tub all you could think of was how he yelled in front of the elementary school, "My blood is on your hands!" before turning around and storming off down the hill. I forgive you that you didn't know as you watched him disappear down the hill that it would be one of his last days. And I forgive you that you didn't take his threat too seriously because he had threatened to take his life many times and you didn't know he meant it this time. I forgive you for not knowing. I forgive you for sitting in that tub and blaming yourself for it all.

Because you did. You blamed yourself for the weight of all of it. For the fact that less than seventy-two hours after he screamed those words, you discovered your body could make sounds you didn't know it could make as two police officers walked up to your front door, after reading a letter that he wrote. A letter blaming you for what he was about to do. I forgive you for sitting in that tub two years later, angry beyond words at the fact that hours before dawn touched the horizon, alone on our lakefront property, he gave up on everything all at once.

It's no wonder you sat in that tub two years later. Think of all you'd endured. Remember the hardest moment of your life? When you had to tell your two children that their father wasn't coming home. The way their eyes actually turned black. That moment, the shape of them, their very essence, faded from their faces, and a light went out for all of you that day. I forgive you for hating him at that moment for causing that.

If I could go back in time to that moment, I'd tell you that you'd make it and that one day it would all be okay. That you'd endure it even if it felt impossible. That not long after losing him you'd sit in the closet with all of your wedding photos spread out around you and that your daughter would walk in. And that even though you wouldn't want her to see your stressed, broken spirit, she'd wrap her arms around you and hold you as you cried. It's then that you'd feel a deepening of your bond, of your connection to one another; an ability for you to be vulnerable and for her to be strong. You'd need that connection to get through that day in the tub and everything that came next.

I'd tell you in my letter that you'd use that exact moment to get you through what was to come. When years later your daughter would walk into your room once again but this time to tell you she'd swallowed two bottles of Advil and tried to end her life. It's in this moment that you'd find your strength again, and after two weeks at Kelowna General Hospital you'd know this was a wake-up call to start talking about mental health, that you needed to stop putting things under the rug, that you needed to do the real work to heal from the traumas that grip us from our childhood. That you needed to be willing to ask for help. Because through that you'd learn that real strength isn't just about doing it all on your own or never showing your vulnerability. It's actually the opposite. True strength is being vulnerable. It is learning to ask. It is saying, I need help, I need you.

I promise you that three years after that moment in the tub, your life will look different. There will still be days that are hard, the guilt of living for yourself will slowly dissipate. Days where you are gripped by grief. And then, there will be days where you're enjoying life fully and so grateful. Like the moment you drove home with your daughter from your mother's funeral. You were driving by the Mara Lakes and the sun was shining and you looked over at her and realized that even though you felt like you had lost everything, you'd actually had it all. In that moment you'd realize you were the wealthiest you'd ever be that day while driving through the mountains, watching her giggle and talk while your son chimed in from the back. Your heart goes there still on dark days.

I love you and I forgive you.

You'll live a good life, I promise. The journey ahead won't always be easy. Grief doesn't fade, but you will learn to carry it with grace. You will learn that it's okay to ask for help. It's okay to lean on others. Vulnerability is not a weakness; it's the purest form of strength.

And one day, you'll realize that after great loss, comes love. You'll have the relationship you always longed for—the one with your kids and the one with yourself. The woman you wanted to save all those years ago is the same woman you love today. And because of that love, you can move forward. Tomorrow will be brighter, and you will be blessed with the warmth of the sun again.

CHANTAAL DOUCET

As a realtor with a deep passion for waterfront properties, Chantaal brings extensive knowledge and personal experience to every transaction. Having owned and sold her own properties on the water, I understand the unique appeal and intricacies of these homes. Beyond her professional life, she is a dedicated parent raising three children, two of whom are still at home, and a proud grandparent. Despite facing personal tragedy with the loss of her late husband, she has found peace and a deep appreciation for life. She is committed to being of service to others and helping them find their own slice of happiness. Find her on Instagram and Facebook under Chantaal Doucet or email her at chantaaldoucet@gmail.com.

I am good, I am worthy, I am lovable and have always been, simply for being me.

CHAPTER 7

Pivot, Leap, Lead

Lisa Moore

grew up thinking that I needed to be successful to be loved, constantly looking outward for validation and approval from others in order to feel like I belonged. I was always striving to succeed to prove that I was worthy; as though my achievements and success were confirmation that I was living a life of purpose. That's how I found myself climbing the corporate ladder in my early thirties, working in an executive position in a large publicly traded company with no work-life balance to speak of and making six figures in sales and marketing while not really living.

At the peak of my career at the age of thirty-five, I became pregnant. I was so intensely focused on my work that I struggled to take the maternity leave I was offered. I didn't want to have the time away from the office and lose all of the financial benefits of continuing to work. In the end, I decided not to take maternity leave at all so I could continue to bring in my salary, but I had difficulty reconciling that decision and was incredibly unhappy. I found myself in a place where I was questioning everything about myself and my role in life. I felt lost and despondent but couldn't understand why. I was married previously and when that marriage failed, I knew I wanted to remarry and have another child, so the fact that I was feeling so unhappy when I finally had what I'd been yearning for for years, was confusing. I felt a lot of guilt and shame, wondering why this newborn baby wasn't bringing me the joy and happiness that society and culture has conditioned us to expect after becoming a mother. I did not realize at the time that these feelings were centered around something much more serious than unhappiness and disconnection.

At the height of my feelings of despondency, my general practitioner referred me to a psychiatrist. I was relieved to learn that my feelings of detachment from the baby were rooted in a diagnosis of postpartum depression. I was also confused. I didn't know a lot about postpartum depression at the time. I just knew that even though mentally I wanted my baby, I felt such a sense of detachment. Because of that, I felt guilty and ashamed and was afraid to share my feelings for fear of being judged or not understood. This made it very difficult for me to ask for help, and is one of the main reasons why so many women suffer from postpartum depression in silence.

It was these dark moments in my life where I realized that I was so distracted by my desire to achieve success that I'd lost sight of what truly mattered. I couldn't see who I could truly be if I allowed myself the freedom to explore more for myself. When the realization hit me, I sat there holding my baby understanding on a very deep level that I didn't want to go back to the life that I'd previously led. The success was simply a mask and a hindrance for me to self-actualize and pursue experiences that could bring me real purpose, joy, and happiness.

Despite this newfound knowledge, I struggled over what to do next. I knew I didn't want to go back to my role in the workplace, but I was a major financial contributor to our family finances. I felt pressured knowing I was counted on, and my children needed the extended health care benefits and financial compensation that my high-level position brought with it. But I couldn't shake the feeling that I'd fundamentally changed and I no longer felt the drive for financial success. In its place was a need to do something different, something real; something that helped others in a meaningful way and that would ultimately also help myself.

Leaning into my inner-knowing, I remember the defining moment where I acknowledged to myself that I was tired of others telling me what they want, and that it's up to me to stand up for myself and tell others what I need. Something in me knew it was time to stand for my convictions and to express my desire for change. And I knew I then needed to act, to make the changes I needed to make in order to move forward and be happy. I was done with the outside world's expectations. At thirty-six years old, I realized I had a choice. And so for the first time in my life, I chose myself. Finally, ME. Being free to make that choice was empowering and so incredibly powerful that it rocked my world and forever changed my destiny.

The steps to my new path weren't always easy and I learned that it required more than making a choice to change. I found myself questioning what would happen if I changed my life and walked away from that corporate lifestyle. Who would I be without the success and money? Would I still be worthy of love? What would happen if I jumped off this cliff, landed in this unknown place? Could I embrace this pivot?

In order to find the courage to walk my new path, I needed to do the spiritual work to heal those parts of me that genuinely believed I was only worthy because of what I had accomplished in my career. I needed to move forward and understand and accept that I deserved to live a life that ignited my passion and fulfilled me. I needed to learn to embrace that I deserved to live the life that I am here to live, and not to live by someone else's rules of what a good life is or what others think my worth is. I had to determine my own value and build self worth.

So began my transformational journey—a spiritual awakening that changed the entire trajectory of my life. At the time I had no idea one small leap would change everything about my life and where I find myself today. It started with therapy, and that process led me to places and parts of me that broke wide open. I was able to work through trauma from my childhood and look at the masks I'd created to hide my pain and sadness. I remember feeling truly authentic and allowing myself to be vulnerable and look at very painful parts of my past. I had to learn to forgive the people who had hurt me and not let trauma define who I wanted to become and the life I wanted for myself and my family. I came to realize that I'd given my power to others and that I needed to come to a place of ownership in my life. Through this work, I was surprised how quickly the leap to healing came when I was truly willing to acknowledge and work through the pain from my past.

My healing experience opened my eyes to the fact that I could use my trauma to help others in need. So, I decided to pursue my Masters in Counselling Psychology and go back to school. In the beginning, the process was daunting as I looked around the room full of 20-year-old students, but still, I squirmed with delight. It was difficult to learn how to study again after not being in school for over twenty years, though. My first exam was a disaster. I had to humbly pick up my pride from the failed grade on the paper and ask for help. I had to learn how to not be in control and I had to resign myself to the process of learning. I was not on my game; I did not know the game, but I had to learn how to play it.

What I hadn't realized until I began the journey of pursuing my master's degree was how robust this particular program was. Pursuing a degree in psychology means you must do your own work. I was forced to continue to work through my childhood trauma and adverse childhood experiences. To strip down my life and look at all the hurt and pain that I'd felt from a small child to adulthood. It meant really looking at myself, my past, taking responsibility for the pain I'd caused others, and making amends for those actions. I was forced to resolve the past so that I could learn to let go of my pain and move forward in my life. It meant being truly vulnerable not only with myself but with my professors and my fellow colleagues. It meant being real, showing all parts of myself: the good, the bad, and the ugly.

My partner had special needs children of his own and while I was completing my Masters program we were learning the system of trying to find resources for his children at the same time. During this time of study and research, I found I was drawn to working with parents of special needs children and advocating for them. I took my own personal experience of trying to find resources for the children and then translated those learnings to help others who so desperately were trying to find their own answers and support for their children. I also discovered that I loved counselling children, so I became a play therapist. I began working with the children and parents and helped many get formal diagnoses, receive access to resources and funding, and to feel supported. I often hear parents tell me it is the first time they have ever spoken to a therapist who understands their struggles and what they face day-to-day raising neurodivergent children.

After opening my own private practice working with families and children, I met my business partner who also had a passion for working with families, but in the context of navigating high conflict separation and divorce. We found that we had synergies in helping families navigate challenging times in their lives. We merged our individual practices together to form a group practice, called Crossroads Collective. It honored where we both came from, and gave us the ability to help more people than we could as individuals. We both embraced the pivot and believed in ourselves when we came to a crossroads in our life. We both felt the challenge and chose to take a different path that honored ourselves. Through our collective practice we found this place, this sweet spot of healing—this place where it really was about learning to advocate, to teach others, and most importantly, choosing ourselves. Choosing our passion. Choosing to listen to our inner mind and heart that we needed to help others to help ourselves.

Looking back, it feels ironic that I was so scared to leave my sales and marketing job only to find myself doing the same type of work now. My business partner and I recognized that she preferred to take on a hands-on clinical role for the organization, whereas I felt the drive to manage the sales and marketing and business-related activities of the organization. We both got to do the work we love administratively all while helping others as we continued to counsel and advocate for our clients when we work face-to-face with them therapeutically. I am now able to meld both worlds together. Only this time, instead of reporting to the corporate ladder, I get to report to myself. I get to write my own rules. I get to decide the hours I work. I get to decide if I work from my home office or whether I work in the clinic. I get to create a life of freedom that I never thought could be possible when I was employed for a corporate conglomerate. I get to enjoy this freedom because I chose to take a risk, I chose myself when I came to a crossroads in my life. I get to have this life because I chose to pivot and to have the courage to leap into the unknown.

The growing, learning, and leading has not stopped and just this year we created a sister organization, Crossroads Collective Learning Institute, where I am now teaching others how to practice play therapy. My business partner is training other therapists how to work with high conflict divorced and separated families. The learning keeps unfolding and the growth comes along with it. We are helping and serving others. We are creating massive ripples of impact for others, who, just like me, were in that dark moment, feeling lost and alone. They know the life that they are living right now is not the life they are meant to be living.

Life throws us many crossroads in our lives. It's my belief and my lived experience that when we're presented with a problem, we can run or hide from the issue or we can use it as an opportunity to gain experience and learn from it. Trusting myself to make a career shift taught me that in every situation, instead of looking at the obstacles as problematic, I can use them as an opportunity to pivot, take a risk and allow myself to leap into the unknown. To trust that if I open myself up to new ideas it has the potential to open doors that lead me to leading a life I'd never dreamed of before.

I look back at my younger self and am so proud of the person I am today because that version of me had the courage to pivot and advocate for her own needs. And from this view, I now have the opportunity and the privilege to step from a place of growth and healing to a place of leadership. Knowing that I am good, I am worthy, I am lovable and have always been, simply for being me. I am honored that I am at a place where I am asking others to come with me on this path of freedom, inviting them to take risks, asking them if they want to pivot too, inviting them to step off the edge and to fly along with me.

LISA MOORE

My story is one shaped by resilience and transformation. I received my BA in Business Administration in 2000, which led to a career in the medical field in senior leadership roles. By 2018, I completed my Master's in Counselling Psychology and opened a counselling group private practice, Crossroads Collective. My love for leadership led to the creation of Crossroads Collective Learning Institute that provides play therapy training for therapists. I have a blended family of five children both neurotypical and neurodiverse. My personal time is spent boating or skiing. My journey reflects a continuous evolution, guided by a desire to learn, grow, and contribute positively to the lives of others. Please feel free to connect with me via email at lisa.crossroadscollective@gmail.com or through my website www.crossroadscollective.ca.

The only change we truly can create is that change within ourselves.

CHAPTER 8

Narcissists CAN Change

Kathryn Morrow

The act of leaving a relationship is a more privileged action than one may think. It's not always that easy. In fact, it rarely is. It's complex and layered. Many women stay for financial reasons, or simply to keep full custody of their children. In some cases, women stay to protect their children because of the potential dangers of their children being raised by the other parent with no protection and supervision. My choice to stay was actually where everything changed.

You see, I grew up in a really good home. Almost as if I grew up in a bubble, where the problems of the outside world couldn't get to me. Unlike a lot of my friends, there was no fighting in my home. I also grew up with a great example of what it was to be husband and wife, and I had a great relationship with my father, so I didn't have the "daddy-issues" that are so commonly spoken about among young women. I remember, as a little girl, skipping to school with really no care in the world, and as I grew older, I had good, solid relationships through my adolescent years. I wasn't trapped in a negative, unhealthy, trauma-bonding pattern of abuse that many women find themselves stuck in and repeating. I had healthy relationships and a healthy sense of self.

Then one day, I met my husband, and boy did he sweep me off my feet. I had never experienced a narcissist or love bombing before, but let me tell you, for a time, that love bombing sure feels sweet. This love is strong and feels incredibly genuine. This kind of love encapsulates you and makes you feel like the only woman on the planet. Without realizing it, this intense love began to slowly isolate me. Bit by bit I let go of my past life and joined my soon-to-be husband on his mission to manipulate and control me.

Unknowingly, I enabled his manipulation, because narcissists wear masks, and until this point, the mask was the only version of him I saw. What I didn't realize was that there was a monster underneath.

"Just leave."

"You don't deserve this."

"Narcissists can't change."

These are some of the things I was told when people found out what my marriage was actually like behind closed doors, in the privacy and secrecy of our home.

And, while I believe these people thought they had my best interests at heart—after all they were coming from a place of love, I believe that society has gotten a little bit lost. There is a very common reality, one that is often sugarcoated to the outside world. Women, and people in general, are suffering in silence. They are afraid to expose the brutality of the emotional abuse that exists in their homes, confused by the masks of narcissism, and embarrassed by the unmet and sometimes forced sexual expectations in the bedroom.

I am no longer hiding. I'm here to give it to you real, raw, and uncensored. Through reading this chapter I want to bring anointed healing to your life—you are not reading this story by accident. I'm here to share my story and my experience about how I truly found a way to stand in my own strength and to take radical responsibility for my life—even though life handed me a tough situation, an unfair situation, a very unexpected situation. When many people around me told me to leave, I stayed. I chose to stay in my relationship with a narcissist.

As I came into this place of choosing; choosing myself, choosing my children, choosing what I truly believed was right for our little family, regardless of what anyone else thought, my choice to stay is what provided the blueprint for my life. This is where my life truly changed. What I wanted was to keep my family together. I didn't believe that two separate homes would be healthier than the home we were trying to build together. I did not want to be a divorce statistic, and I refused to succumb to society's idea that leaving was healthier than staying.

Not long after we started our relationship, we got married. After all, we were madly in love, why wait? The thing is, once that ring was on my finger, the love bombing turned into abuse. I started to feel stuck. It was tumultuous for years; there was emotional, spiritual, physical, and even sexual abuse. I remember the moment I realized something was really wrong. Like many women, I justified and explained his behavior because I had been enabling it all along. I blamed myself and thought if I could act a certain way, treat him a certain way, or give him more sex, I could manage his emotions and reactions...but I was wrong.

One day we were in an argument, which was the norm in our home. Not a day would go by that he didn't yell and I didn't cry, but this argument was different. I was used to the name calling. I expected the yelling. I even got used to the dirty looks, sneers, and other negative body language. But today, things escalated. He was holding a freshly brewed cup of black coffee—hot coffee, and in his frustration he stuck his hand in his mug and attempted to splash it into my face. Thankfully, it didn't burn me. The act of sticking his hand in there and splashing it cooled the coffee long before it got to me, but the intent was there. Although he ended up burning himself, his intent was to burn me. This was the first act of physical intimidation that I remember, and there were many to follow but still, I did not leave. My husband scared me, but something in me kept me from leaving. Some say it was a trauma bond, but I still believe it was love.

As we continued in our rocky marriage, we decided to have children, which was one of the deepest desires of my heart. Some people might call me crazy for wanting to have a family with a man I was sometimes afraid of, but like so many women—like SO MANY families, we took that next step despite our volatile home life. I remember the moment when I first discovered I was pregnant. I was sitting there looking at the line on the pregnancy test, and I had this awakening that I was carrying another life inside of me, that we had just created a family unit that was beyond just me and my husband. While staring at that line, there became this conviction within me that I would do all that I could to create a safe, secure, stable, and healthy home for this little one. What I wasn't aware of at the time was that this little one was actually two. We were having twins.

As I first held my babies in my arms, I felt stuck in that moment. There was this pause, this moment of regret: how could I do this? How could I bring two innocent, beautiful little girls into a world of contempt? Before I could give much energy to these negative and unwelcome thoughts, a wave of relief washed over me and I felt a strong confirmation that these little girls were, indeed, always meant to be ours. That this was the right decision and that everything was going to be okay.

Let's Not Sugarcoat It

I had truly come into an emotional space that no matter how bad it got, I was committed to creating the change in our home, for our babies, our beautiful children, and my family. It wasn't until I got pregnant with our third child that it became obvious to me that I needed to do more in order to live the life I wanted.

When I discovered our unborn baby was a boy, I remember looking at his ultrasound photo and realizing, more than ever, that I needed to break the cycle. Although we had made some positive changes in our home, I knew there must be more we could do. It's then that I decided to take even more responsibility for how I showed up, because in the abuse I suffered from my husband, I had become reactively abusive back.

I could see that my reactions, the defensiveness, contempt, and stonewalling, were perpetuating the abuse cycle. All I really wanted to do was focus on myself and my children to create a loving bond, safety, and connection. I actually had no desire left to fix what was broken in my marriage, but I knew that I didn't want my sweet babies in his presence alone fifty percent of the time, which would have been the result of divorce, so I chose to save my marriage in order to save and protect my children.

What happened next was absolutely magical, because the sacrifice I made for my kids, my dedication to keep my family together, resulted in the most beautiful byproduct; I got my husband back. It didn't happen overnight, but as we welcomed our third child into our family, I started to come from a place of understanding. I started seeing my husband as a young boy who was traumatized, and I had a new empathy for the way that he grew up, which created an unhealthy dynamic in his life, and subsequently our lives. I started to see our relationship from a different perspective. I started to honor his process while still respecting my boundaries. I learned how to stand in my own strength to lead my husband, and my whole family, through the trauma and the healing, to a place of fighting the stigma of divorce, where we could have what we both wanted—a healthy, safe, loving home and family.

What I know now is that if more of us dedicate ourselves to a "no matter what" mindset, if we choose to live out our vows until death do us part, there would be far fewer broken homes and families, and we would be able to foster much healthier connections, relationships, and opportunities. If we could adopt this mindset, collectively, more people would believe and know that they could get through anything by choosing themselves.

Choosing yourself doesn't always mean leaving; it can actually mean—just like in my story— staying.

I am so grateful that I chose to stay. Though it was a hard road, we have now had four years of a beautiful connection and marriage that we would have walked away from. My twins would have two homes, and my little boy might not even exist.

My husband showed up to do the work because I showed up for my relationship with my children. By seeing my husband as the little boy who had been hurt, I came to a place of being able to love him through his trauma and accept him as he was. By choosing to better myself and our family unit, I unexpectedly invited him into an exploration of himself and sent us all on a journey I couldn't have even imagined.

Ultimately, the only change we truly can create is that change within ourselves. When we learn to truly lead ourselves by standing in our own strength, then, just like for me, the beautiful byproduct, is often that others follow your lead.

I am grateful now to watch my husband leading other men who are coming into that beautiful healing experience that men need to be seen, to be witnessed, to be heard, and to be held through their own traumas. I am leading women to do the same, so that we can both show up in our connections, in our relationships, and in our friendships, from a place that is not full of triggers and trauma, but from a place of understanding and openness; a place where we choose ourselves while also choosing each other. Because that, my friend, is what it's truly about.

I believe each of us has the power to change our situations. If my narcissistic husband can shift and change, then I know anyone can grow and evolve, but we have to want it badly enough. We have to be willing to take responsibility for our choices, for our reactions, for how we see and perceive the relationship, the world around us, the places we find ourselves in, and the challenges we are facing. It is that perspective, and also in this conviction, that brings us into a deeper place of commitment to our goals and dreams. It is in this conviction that you can gain the strength to stand up for what you want for your life—whatever that is for you—and no one outside of you gets to tell you what that looks like.

Whether you are facing a crossroads in your relationship, where you're questioning if you should stay or go, or whether it's a job or a business, I want to ask you, have you gone all in? Do you have a conviction in your heart that you are committed to this no matter what? Do you really believe in the vows you gave, until death do us part, or are you always one foot out the door with a backup plan?

For myself, if I'd had a back up plan, and if I was not all in, then when my tough situation arose that was unfair, traumatic, and even abusive, I might have abandoned ship and we may have missed out on an amazing opportunity for love and growth—for myself, my husband, and our marriage. I recognized that my situation was just that, a situation, and I did not have to accept it as my reality. I knew I could make a change.

I stood in my strength and took control of my relationship in three ways. I Didn't Get on the "Crazy Train." The "Crazy Train" is a term I coined when I started coaching women in toxic relationships. For me, it symbolizes the moment when my husband began to lose control—through contempt, criticism, blame, name-calling, or some other form of attack. I realized I had a choice. I could fight back, fueling the cycle of attack and defense, or I could recognize the situation for what it was—a loss of control and composure. By choosing to maintain my own composure and control my reaction, I stayed off the Crazy Train. I learned that if I leaned into defensiveness, things would spiral out of control, and before long, I'd be right there on the train, lacking control and composure, just like my husband. Worse, I'd find myself driving that train, heading nowhere good and turning into a rollercoaster. To avoid that, I chose to steer clear of the Crazy Train.

I also recognized and knew the signs of a "Narc-Out." Another term I created, the "Narc-Out," represents an extreme version of the Crazy Train. Whether or not my husband was a full-blown narcissist, I realized that many people carry "Cluster B" personality traits, such as those linked to Narcissistic Personality Disorder, Borderline Personality Disorder, Histrionic Personality Disorder, and Antisocial Personality Disorder. These traits can lead to cognitive distortions and alternate realities. When my husband was on the verge of a Narc-Out, I noticed that his emotional responses became extreme and often didn't make sense. He would repeat himself, assuming I didn't hear him, all while claiming that I wasn't listening, didn't understand, and didn't care. He would also twist what I said, hearing things I never said. His distorted reality, rooted in trauma, caused him to see and hear things that didn't exist. In these moments, I realized it wasn't me against him—it was the two of us against his distorted reality. Instead of arguing or defending myself, I'd calmly state, "we both know that's not true," which helped bring us back to the same team as my husband slowly came back to reality.

Lastly, I led with empathy and provided reality checks. In my experience, cognitive distortions in abusive relationships can cause a lot of conflict. When I found out our third child was a boy, I felt motivated to raise him to become a strong man—a man who would not only know how to treat a woman but also know how to love and accept himself. By thinking of this little boy, I channeled my love and redirected it to my husband. I reminded myself that he, too, was once a little boy, likely carrying trauma from that time. Leading with empathy meant putting aside my own agenda and trying to understand what it was like for him. When I led with empathy, I created a deep connection between us, which allowed me to softly help him see and identify his distortions. Reality checking, for me, meant showing or telling my husband what was actually happening in the moment when he was getting triggered and his reality was being skewed. The longer I showed up with empathy, the easier and more accepted these reality checks became, shifting me from adversary to trusted confidant, rooted in love, empathy, and truth.

In closing, I learned to take radical responsibility for my life, my choices, my perspective, and the way I handled myself. Instead of living in a reactive state, I chose to live with intention and strength.

In Jesus' Name

KATHRYN MORROW

Kathryn Morrow and her family currently reside in San Antonio, Texas where Kathryn is passionate about her relationship with Jesus, home-schooling, and running her little hobby farm. She is the founder and CEO of The White Picket Fence Project, a program designed to help women stand in their own power and strength to avoid divorce and keep their families together. By arming women with the tools to manage conflict, she and her husband have helped over 4400 marriages calm the chaos and reconnect deeply in love. For more information, or to connect with Kathryn, visit whitepicketfenceproject.com or find her on Instagram @kathrynmorrowonline. Kathryn has also written the foreword for her husband's book, Disrupting Divorce, which can be purchased at newrockpress.com/dd or on Amazon.

Now I was holding on to the moments, rather than the memories.

CHAPTER 9

Rising From the Ashes

Carien Rennie

There are defining moments in life; moments that compel us to burn everything down, let it all go, and start anew. These are the difficult moments in life, those that are out of our control, when we have to rely on faith to bring us through to the lessons. These moments have brought me to my knees and forced me to reevaluate what truly matters, ultimately offering me a new perspective on life. But all of the prior trauma and challenges of my life seemed insignificant the moment I found myself facing a trauma so profound it would shape my entire existence.

I'd experienced a lot of trauma in my twenty-three years, pain and loss in so many areas of my life, from partners, best friends, and family, and the words of my step-grandmother still ringing in my ears, "You don't belong in this family, you are the bastard child of another man," knowing that it wasn't even the worst of it. It was betrayal, rejection, hatred, and complete disregard on the highest level..

The recurring patterns of abuse in my life kept surfacing, leaving me feeling trapped and utterly stuck. I felt like I met the creator of these absurd patterns and expectations the day I met my soon-to-be father-in-law. Never had I ever met a more bitter man in my life. This guy just hated my guts before he even met me. Nothing would ever be good enough for his precious son, whom he treated like shit sometimes. It did not mean that I just moved past it like someone else might do. No, I festered in it, made it mean something it should not, and felt hurt and betrayed by his actions for so many years. I felt responsible to keep my partner happy, such a false sense of responsibility strapped to my back passed on by generations, a backpack so heavy no one should carry. His son chose me anyway and in some ways I

97

feel that made him resent me even more.

My fiancé and I had been living together for a couple of months and had recently moved to his dad's acreage of land. The financial help was welcomed and presented to us so early on in our relationship when we didn't have a lot of money and saving every penny was very helpful so we could build a life together. Living in a home on his land was miserable. Although we had our own house it never felt like it was ours nor did we have any privacy. I have never felt more depressed and out of control of my life as I did living there.

One night there was a particularly fierce storm with lightning illuminating the sky and thunder shaking the walls of our home. That storm, it felt like, was a reflection of what I felt on the inside. That day was yet another when I felt helpless with my circumstances and just life in general. I'd just put our one-year-old son to bed, his tiny chest rising and falling with each peaceful breath, oblivious to the chaos outside. My fiancé was soaking in the bathtub, unwinding after a long day. I could hear the water sloshing gently as he moved, the only sound in the house other than the storm.

My mother's voice echoed in my mind telling me not to be in the bath during a lightning storm, a piece of wisdom ingrained from childhood. Nervously, I crept into the bathroom. "Perhaps you should come to bed," I suggested, trying to mask my anxiety. "It's not safe to be in the water during a storm." He chuckled, brushing off my concerns. "What's the chance of lightning striking our house," he asked, his tone dismissive.

I left him there and climbed into bed, pulling the covers up to my chin to wait for my fiancé. Just as we started to drift off, a blinding flash of light filled the room, followed by a deafening roar. I bolted upright, my heart pounding. The house had been struck by lightning. I panicked, the first thing that came into my mind was that the burglar bars had just been reinforced and could now trap us inside.

I could see smoke almost immediately. Panic surged through me, but there was no time to waste. We leapt out of bed, he yelled at me to get our son, and I ran to our son's room, while he was looking where we could escape. The smoke made a clear barrier at our son's open door, but inside his room, the air was still clear. I grabbed him, wrapping him in a blanket to shield him from the smoke, and raced back into the corridor.

My fiancé met me there, his face pale. Thick, acrid smoke filled the air, making it hard to see, hard to breathe. He threw another blanket over me, tucked us under his arm, and we ran through the smoke, heading for the only exit we could think of. We made it in mere seconds before the steel and glass door, and our only exit point, was too hot to be touched.

We burst out into the open air, gasping for breath. Behind us, our home was engulfed in flames. The thatched roof, dry as tinder, had caught fire immediately. Getting our son somewhere safe was our first priority. His aunt, who also lived on the property, took our son to safety so we could try to get some of our belongings out. Frozen, I wondered how I was supposed to decide what was most important. We tried to rescue what we could, but eventually, we just stood there, helpless, watching everything we owned get consumed by the fire. I turned and looked at the small safe that carried our important documents and a small heap of whatever was grabbed, and I knew that was it; that was all that was left.

These moments in life have a way to either propel us to transformational change or break us. The question I kept asking myself over and over again was whether I was going to use this situation as a catalyst to inspire me to grow into something bigger and better in the future or if I was going to feel sorry for myself and stay right where I was. My dad had wisdom, no warmth or emotional connectedness, but I learned a lot from him. I knew he loved me, but I desired the connection more than anything. I was just such an angry teenager that I thought I was unlovable, and if we are going through life looking for evidence that we don't belong, we will find it. He always said: "You need to fall to learn, the secret lies in getting up. Never stay down." That night when my house was engulfed in flames my father kept saying over and over that it's only stuff and that stuff is not important. Deep down I knew my father had such an open hand and trying to keep up with others made him feel just as exhausted as me.

The first few weeks after the fire were some of the hardest of my life. Our immediate concern was survival. We needed the basics: food, clothing, a roof over our heads. Thinking back, those were some of the happiest times in our relationship, together on the floor of this small apartment. We did not have much, but we had more than we needed. It was at night that my worries caught up with me, when the silence crept in and I could hear my own thoughts; those were the scary times. It solidified all the bad thoughts I had about myself. I had the running internal dialogue of how I deserved what happened because I was such an unlovable person, and how life is just not fair, or that bad things always happen to me. I get it. I was going through a shitty thing that honestly I had no idea to navigate, like most of the big things that happened in my life. Do we ever really know? We'd lost everything in the fire that day—the table my mother had given me, family photos, all our physical possessions. Still I found myself constantly questioning: what was worse, the physical losses or the emotional impact?

Realizing that you have nothing tangible to go along with the memory, no picture or keepsake to even represent the life we had before we moved in together, takes an emotional toll on you. I can't ever get those tangible links back. I soon realized that those were only material possessions, they would mean nothing without the people. My perspective changed and now I was holding on to the moments, rather than the memories. How many times was I so busy trying to capture the perfect moment in a photo that I completely missed the moment itself? How many of these moments have gone by in my life when I wasn't paying enough attention?

But in that loss, something miraculous happened. As we sat on that blanket in our bare apartment, I realized what truly mattered. It wasn't the things we had lost; it was the moments we had shared, the love we had for each other, our son, the gratitude I had in my heart that we were all safe. My dad's words that he said the night we watched our house burn down were repeating in my mind:. "Stuff can be replaced, what matters is that you are all safe."

Living in a small apartment with almost nothing was a stark contrast to the life we had known before the fire. We slept on a mattress on the floor and ate off makeshift tables. But I soon learned there was a strange sense of freedom in this simplicity we had in our lives now. With all the distractions stripped away, we were forced to confront the core of our existence—not only each other, but our deepest selves. I had to ask myself some very hard questions. Was the life I was living before the fire what I really wanted? I felt deeply uninspired and unmotivated. I felt defeated by life. Those are some pretty big feelings to deal with in your early twenties. I didn't think that it would be possible to have a better life than the one that I was living, than the one that I'd grown up in, nor did I think I deserved that in a million years. But I knew that if I wanted that, I would have to do things differently.

Even before the fire, my fiancé and I had been through a lot. Our relationship had been strained, especially living under the watchful, controlling eye of his father. One year into our relationship my fiancé chose to cheat on me. The betrayal cut really deep, the wound eventually healed, but the scars were there. I stayed with him after the betrayal—everyone deserves a second chance, was what I kept saying. The reality is, I knew back then. I knew I should not have married him, yet I chose to do it anyway. I did love him, but two broken people don't make one whole relationship. Everything had to be done the way my soon to be father-in-law stipulated. He was controlling and disrespectful and it took me years to break free from it. He was very good to us financially, helping to reduce our rent to a bare minimum. I never wanted to go live in the house that burned down in the first place, but we were so young and we needed the money. It came at such a high price, though, like everything he did for us. I was made very aware of the fact that if he did something for us it was only for his son. He was rude and dismissive, a sexist in every sense of the word.

The fire, in a strange twist of fate, freed us from that environment. It was a chance to rebuild, not just our home, but our relationship, as a couple and a new family, away from judgment and control of my father-in-law. The fire gave a chance to face the demons that had been chasing us individually for years. I was carrying a lot of resentment, bitterness, rejection, and anger. I had so much anger that it consumed me. I was angry that my biological father was an alcoholic, that my stepfather only took care of us out of obligation, and that although my stepfather was a great guy, there was no depth and no emotion from him. My list of things to be angry about was so long that I just permanently stayed angry. I didn't even know why I was angry anymore. I had to sit in that anger long enough until I realized it was actually covering sadness.

Looking back now, one of the many lessons I learned and applied to my life, was in order to rebuild the literal and metaphorical house, the faulty foundations needed to be re-done. I had to go back to my emotional foundations and ask myself some hard questions. What did all of this mean? What was true about me that I was telling myself and why? I had to take that information piece by piece and dissect it like a fish with way too many bones. I had to look at what was true in the beliefs that I was carrying and what were just stories I told myself. That was the start of a very intense journey of learning many lessons. I knew I had to start facing the problems, taking the scenarios, and really working through them. Looking at my low self esteem, my feelings of unworthiness. I truly felt ugly and unlovable and like a complete loser. I felt like I wasted my life and it was over. I had such a limited capacity back then.

Let's Not Sugarcoat It

This time was filled with a lot of journaling, crying, and screaming. Doing the things that I felt I needed to do and feeling the emotions as they came up and not just stuffing down the tears instead of letting them go. I needed to let the tears flow to finally cleanse my soul. Many days I just broke down and cried. I screamed so much into my pillow that the sadness I left behind was tangible. I had to take a hard, long look at the things that put me, Carien, together. What were the thoughts and patterns that were life as I knew it? I knew that this burning house might as well just have been my heart and emotional state. This house was me in a metaphorical sense. It was time to rebuild my "home," because the one that burned down was just a house. This horrible time turned out to be one of the greatest masters in my life.

The fire had taken everything we owned, but in its wake, it gave us something invaluable—a deep sense of community and overwhelming generosity. We learned to value the simple, meaningful aspects of life, realizing that it wasn't about material possessions, but the love and support of those around us. The community rallied in ways that left us speechless with gratitude, with friends, neighbors, and even strangers offering clothes, food, and money. Their kindness was humbling and transformative, opening my heart to the importance of giving and the joy of helping others. One moment that stands out was when a neighbor, someone we barely knew, brought over clothes and toys for our son, moving me to tears. This experience taught me the true power of community and left me more empathetic, compassionate, and committed to giving back in any way I could.

From that point on, I made a commitment to live with a giving heart. If I didn't need something, I gave it away. I learned that holding onto things was pointless; what truly mattered was sharing what we had with those in need. This philosophy of generosity became a guiding principle in my life, shaping who I am today. After the fire I began to see the world differently. It was like a small crack appeared in a very big wall that had been built to guard my heart. The material possessions we accumulate can vanish in an instant, but the memories we create and the love we share are what truly matter. It's taking advantage of being in the moment, being present, not just physically, but also mentally and emotionally. This profound realization shifted my entire outlook on life.

Sometimes I still find myself caught up in the hustle and bustle of life, always looking ahead, always planning for the future. But the fire taught me the importance of slowing down, of appreciating the present moment. It made me realize that life is fleeting, and that we should make the most of the time we have with our loved ones. Every challenge and setback is an opportunity to redefine our paths, deepen our connections, and discover our true selves.

The fire was a defining moment in my life for other reasons, as well. It forced me to confront my fears, to find strength in the face of adversity. It showed me that I was capable of more than I ever imagined. I learned that I could rebuild, that I could start over, and that I could thrive even after losing everything. When I face adversaries now I always remind myself that I have overcome this hard thing, looked into the face of the demons I was carrying with me, and rebuilt my foundation. Remembering that gives me strength to carry on.

This experience also deepened my faith. Growing up in a Christian home, faith had always been a part of my life. But the fire brought it to the forefront. I found myself turning to prayer, seeking comfort and guidance. And in those moments of quiet reflection, I felt a sense of peace and assurance that everything would be okay. Faith became my anchor, my source of strength. It gave me the courage to face each new day, to tackle each new challenge. It reminded me that even in the darkest times, there is always a glimmer of hope, a light that guides me forward.

CARIEN RENNIE

Originally from the vibrant landscapes of South Africa, Carien Rennie now calls Kelowna home, bringing her dynamic spirit and rich life experiences to the community. After managing accounts for a local upmarket lifestyle magazine, Carien has now embarked on an exciting journey in real estate. However, the role she cherishes most is being a proud mom to her three amazing boys, aged 15, 18, and 21.

Carien is passionate about connecting with people and believes deeply in the power of community. She's a strong advocate for personal growth, living by the belief that we're all on a lifelong journey of self-improvement. She lives her daily life according to her mantra: be the change you want to see in others. She loves to share and connect, so feel free to reach out to her on Instagram @carienrennie or Facebook at Carien Rennie.

The experiences I've had have shaped who I am, but they do not define me.

CHAPTER 10

Beyond the Shadows: A Journey of Courage and Recovery

Heidi Johnson

As a child, there was nothing I craved more than my father's love and attention. I wanted him to praise me, choose to spend time with me, and shower me with love and affection. Today I can see how I allowed the belief that I wasn't chosen or loved by my father to shape my existence. Eventually, that longing for love and attention manifested in my romantic relationships and profoundly influenced my life.

Looking back, much of my life has felt like a ceaseless battle for acknowledgment; a struggle that traces back to my upbringing with an alcoholic father who was often emotionally distant and preoccupied. The fracture of my parents' marriage when I was seven, deepened the feeling of inadequacy. To my seven year old self I felt that I was being replaced in my father's affections by his new family with his new girlfriend.

Despite knowing my father harbored love for me, I perpetually struggled with an inner conviction of not measuring up, relentlessly striving to earn his approval. In the chaos of turmoil, my mother assumed both parenting roles, tirelessly working to provide the support and care that my father could not. Her strength and unwavering dedication have been the cornerstone of my ability to navigate and overcome the many challenges I have faced in my life.

So let me bare my soul: the pain of growing up with a father battling his own demons, the anguish of enduring rape at sixteen, the agony of staying in an unloving and unfaithful relationship for sixteen years, all because of our beautiful daughters. I won't sugarcoat it, none of these experiences are okay. They cut deep and have left scars that have never fully healed.

At sixteen I was raped by a boy who I went to school with. After the rape, I felt a profound sense of shame and isolation. Unable to confide in anyone or face the boy when I returned to school that fall, I left my mother's home to live with my father and his new family out of sheer embarrassment. I felt a deep guilt for abandoning my mom because I wasn't strong enough to face the boy who violated me. The weight of my silence and the fear of judgment kept me from seeking the support I desperately needed.

Another challenge came twenty years later, when I made the difficult decision to leave my first marriage. We'd been married for thirteen years and together for eighteen, and for years I'd felt the agony of staying in an unloving and unfaithful relationship for our beautiful daughters. I loved him, but not in that all encompassing full-blown chemistry way, and leaving that thirteen year marriage brought me a sense of peace.

Then, a short year later, I found myself in a new relationship, one that seemed to fill the void of love I'd always craved. It felt intoxicating, like a dream come true. My new partner showered me with love and attention and suddenly it felt like all the affection I'd craved in my first marriage and carried over with me from childhood was being served to me on a silver platter. But in my desire to feel worthy, I failed to recognize that such excessive affection could be a characteristic of narcissism. The intense love and attention I got were not signs of genuine affection but rather tactics of manipulation that eventually led to physical violence. I was being love-bombed, a common strategy used by narcissists to control and dominate their partners.

Eventually, we got married, and our home continued to descend into chaos and violence. Looking back, I was so love-struck that I failed to fully recognize or acknowledge the warning signs, though somewhere deep down, I sensed them. That inner voice tried to speak up, but the little girl within me desperately craved his validation and affection, which he readily provided—until things took a darker turn descending into manipulation. His weapon of choice was love, and I yearned for it so desperately that I would do anything to have it. Even if it meant sacrificing the well-being of my own children. Another warning sign emerged when he said that my own children weren't welcome in our home. The haunting truth that I let it all happen still weighs on me. I feel a deep sense of guilt for the lost years with my girls because I allowed his decisions to control our lives. I resent that I relinquished my power to him, and that, instead of making choices that prioritized my well-being and that of my family, I let him take the lead.

Due to the verbal and physical abuse I was experiencing at home, I sought therapy for our entire relationship in an attempt to cope with the turmoil at home. It's peculiar really, that I don't place sole blame on him for the turbulence in our relationship and have come to acknowledge my own complicity in perpetuating this cycle, relentlessly chasing after his ever-shifting expectations like a mirage on the horizon. Each time I met his demands, they seemed to morph into something new, leaving me feeling like I was endlessly pursuing an elusive finish line. I always questioned myself, wondering if it was something I did that caused him to shift from showering me with affection to subjecting me to verbal and physical attacks. Despite the gnawing realization deep within my gut that our dynamic was unsustainable, the weight of having yet another failed marriage left me grappling with a profound sense of inadequacy and failure.

Then came a day I will never forget. After yet another tumultuous argument erupted within the confines of our home, I found myself in dire need of an escape, a break to sift through the tangled mess that had become my life. I turned to running, seeking comfort in the steady rhythm of my footsteps on the pavement. As my heartbeat steadied and my breathing calmed, I hoped that the physical exertion would grant me a moment of reprieve and mental clarity amidst the chaos. But that day, I couldn't settle my anxiety. So, I ran for what seemed like hours, pushing myself further with each step, hoping to outrun my worries and fears. Looking back, I realize it was another red flag that I had swept under the rug, a sign of the deep unrest that I had ignored for far too long.

As I was on my way back home, starting my cool down, I was suddenly attacked by a stranger I had passed on my path. He attacked me from behind, knocking the wind out of me. When I got my bearings, I realized I was being dragged into the bush by my hair. I remember the fear and sheer panic that set in... "Please, God, don't let me be raped again," I prayed. He was so strong and had somehow gotten bailing twine around my neck, strangling me as he attempted to rape me. In a moment of sheer terror, I fought back with all my strength. By the grace of God, I somehow managed to escape relatively unharmed.

Panicked and desperate for safety, I fled to a nearby creek and hid there, trembling and in shock, until darkness fell. Every sound and movement around me heightened my fear, but I stayed hidden, praying for the ordeal to end. Once it was safe, under the cover of night, I cautiously made my way to a neighbor's house. I was shaken to my core, yet grateful to be alive and to have found sanctuary in the midst of such a horrifying experience.

The police brought me home, and the memory of vulnerability and humiliation still lingers because I had to undress while the police collected my clothing for evidence and photographed my bruises, some from the recent attack, others from past incidents at home. Trembling with fear, I realized I had nowhere safe to escape to. And deep down, I knew this ordeal would somehow be twisted to make it seem like it was my fault.

When the police left, I lowered myself into the bath, the water gradually clouding the water with brown hues and scattered leaves. My husband remained perched on the edge of the tub, his words ringing with accusation. "If you didn't feel the need to go for a run," he coldly stated, "this never would have happened." His words hung heavy in the air, casting a pall over the already tense atmosphere, as I struggled to comprehend the depths of his indifference and blame. Heading home should have been a return to sanctuary, a place to fall apart, express myself, and find safety and love. But even within the walls of my own home, fear gripped me. I was left battered and bruised by someone who was supposed to cherish me. How could I even begin to comprehend or process the trauma of this stranger's attack while simultaneously enduring the relentless assaults within the supposed safety of my own home?

Six days passed and the haunting memories of my attack by the stranger still lingered, casting a shadow over my every move. Then, in the eerie quiet of my home, I found myself facing another terrifying ordeal when suddenly my head crashed against the floor, narrowly missing our coffee table. My husband's grip tightened, holding my face down with a vice-like force, and a surge of panic gripped my entire being. With each agonizing moment, the memories of the attack by the stranger flooded back and merged with the one I was facing at the hands of my husband, amplifying the fear coursing through my veins. Despite my desperate pleas and cries for help, the sense of helplessness overwhelmed me, leaving me paralyzed with terror.

Following the assault, my husband's words pierced through the silence as he callously uttered, "I don't know why you make me do this to you," leaving me stunned and bewildered by his lack of remorse. That day, he had herniated three of my disks in my lower back from the blunt force.

Despite the physical and emotional pain, I continued to stay for two more agonizing years. The man whom I loved, supported, and dedicated my life to had become the source of my torment. I lived in a beautiful home in a gated community, and yet each day felt like an eternity as I found myself trapped in a relentless cycle of anguish and despair, grappling with the harsh reality of my shattered dreams and broken trust.

For two more years, a deep sense of loneliness and grief consumed me, leaving me struggling to find solace from the turmoil. I remember vividly the moment of contemplating taking my own life. I was in the tub again, and feeling as if there was no other way to end the suffering that had become my daily existence. The weight of my emotions was unbearable, and I longed for a sense of peace that seemed forever out of reach. As the water in the bathtub turned cold, I found myself lost in thoughts of how I could end it all. But even in my darkest moment, it was my daughters who ultimately saved me. The thought of having more time with them, being present for them as they navigated through adulthood, pulled me back from the brink. I realized I didn't want to miss out on witnessing their marriages, the births of their babies, or being there for them during life's challenges. If I went through with it, they would be deprived of my presence for the rest of their lives, and I couldn't bear the thought of that.

In that pivotal moment, I made a different choice. I recognized that there was always a way out, and I decided to leave. I packed my bag in the middle of the night and fled my home. With only an overnight bag and my dog, I sought refuge with a friend. I stayed there until I was able to secure a place of my own. Those initial days were filled with uncertainty and fear, not only for my safety but also for my financial future. He had control of everything. He had crippled my business, which left me feeling vulnerable and anxious. However, there was also a sense of hope and determination. I truly believed that I would be dead if I stayed, either by his hands or my own. It was a difficult decision, but I knew it was necessary for my well-being and the future I envisioned for myself and my girls.

After securing a new place, I found my way back to my girls, and they came back to live with me. The reunion was emotional, and we faced many challenges as we worked to rebuild our lives together. It took time to build that trust again and to create that element of love and forgiveness with myself and for them to forgive me. We had to navigate through the pain and the healing process, step-by-step.

Let's Not Sugarcoat It

In those months after leaving my home and my husband, I learned the true meaning of resilience and the power of starting over. I had to forgive myself for the past and prove to my girls that I could be the stable and loving mother they deserved. Through patience, open communication, and countless moments of vulnerability, we began to heal. Each day brought new opportunities for growth and understanding, strengthening the bond between us. I eventually had back surgery, which left me with lifelong mobility issues, but I didn't care. I was a survivor, and I was on a path to a new life.

My daughters and I created new routines, found joy in simple moments, and supported each other through the ups and downs. The journey wasn't easy, but it was worth every effort. Looking back, I am grateful for the strength it took to leave and the courage to rebuild. My relationship with my daughters is now stronger than ever, filled with love, trust, and mutual respect. This experience has shown me the importance of perseverance and the incredible capacity for forgiveness and healing within all of us.

And, in a surprise twist of faith, through all of the upheaval and healing in my own life, my father was able to conquer his own demons. His recovery was unexpected and his love and support became a crucial part of my own healing journey. He transformed from a figure of pain to one of strength, offering the understanding and encouragement I had longed for since I was a child. His recovery taught me that it is possible to overcome even the deepest wounds and that love can be a powerful force for redemption.

The experiences I've had in this lifetime have shaped who I am, but they do not define me. I have found strength in vulnerability, and through the love and support of my mother and father, I have learned to navigate the complexities of life with resilience and grace. Their unwavering dedication has been my anchor, allowing me to rebuild and find a sense of peace and self-worth.

Slowly, I acknowledged the choices I made, the fears I clung to, and the patterns I allowed to persist. And from a place of trust and forgiveness, I began to transform, realizing that true healing comes from within and that embracing our vulnerabilities is the first step toward liberation. As I journeyed through my healing process, I began to cultivate new beliefs about myself, about love, about relationships, and about men. I embarked on a profound exploration of my inner landscape, seeking to understand the roots of my patterns and behaviors. With each revelation, I gained clarity and insight into the dynamics that kept me ensnared in abusive situations.

Through this self-reflection, I recognized the subtle and harmful nature of codependency and the ways in which it influenced my choices. I confronted the uncomfortable truths about my past decisions, acknowledging the role they played in perpetuating my suffering. Yet, instead of dwelling in self-blame, I embraced these realizations as opportunities for growth and transformation. Armed with this newfound awareness, I embarked on a journey of self discovery and empowerment. I learned to trust my instincts and honor my worth, refusing to settle for anything less than the love and respect I deserved. With each step forward, I embraced the power of choice and the ability to create a life rooted in authenticity and self love. From this place of newfound belief, I embarked on a journey of healing and liberation, reclaiming my power and forging a path towards a brighter future.

This journey of transformation has been both beautiful and enriching. It has unfolded in ways that surpass my wildest imagination, opening me up to new experiences and insights that have enriched my life beyond measure. For every moment that has brought me to this point, I am filled with gratitude. Each trial and triumph has played a role in shaping the person I am today, and for that, I am truly thankful.

Reflecting on my journey, I realize that it is not just about the destination but the path I have chosen to take. Each step forward has been an opportunity for growth, a chance to embrace the unknown with courage and curiosity. And as I continue along this path, I am filled with anticipation for the adventures that lie ahead.

As I look back, I see a trail of perseverance, hope, and growth. Each obstacle has been a lesson, each victory a testament to my willpower. The journey has taught me that healing is not a destination but a continuous process, and every experience, no matter how challenging, contributes to the intricate mosaic of who I am becoming. Ultimately, this journey has not only been about personal growth but also about embracing life's infinite possibilities with an open heart and mind. The future is a canvas of endless possibilities, guided by God, and I am eager to see where this path of transformation will lead me next.

HEIDI JOHNSON

Heidi Johnson is the proud mom of two amazing daughters who have grown up to be strong, successful women. In my free time, I love dancing, reading, hiking, swimming, and scuba diving. I'm a foodie at heart and enjoy exploring new cuisines. I cherish moments with my fur babies, who bring so much joy to my life. My biggest accomplishment is not only raising my daughters but also reclaiming my freedom and embracing life on my own terms. These experiences have shaped me into a resilient and passionate individual, always eager to connect with my community and inspire others. Connect with me at linkdin.com/in/heidi-johnson-5673b9b3 and Instagram @heidi.johnson21.

Reframing is not settling.

CHAPTER 11

Reset. Realize. Reframe. Recommit.

Erica Bearss

Traveling home from Thailand, I heard the screeching of brakes and the crashing of glass. Before that could register, I was flying through the windshield of a car and slamming into the concrete wall of a school. Then, total blackout. Those sounds, that moment, I will never forget. But most of what came next, and a lot of what came before, is gone forever.

I was in a taxi heading to the airport after finishing my first Ironman race and the driver of that little red car fell asleep at the wheel. The next thing I knew, I was waking up in a hospital bed ten days later, with no feeling in my right arm, a crushed thorax, and broken ribs. When I finally opened my eyes to what looked like country fog at night, I was greeted with the words "severe brain injury." When I went to reply, to tell them, "No, I'm okay..." No words came out, no matter how hard I tried. This was the moment my life changed. I went from this driven, successful woman to a woman lying in bed broken on so many levels, unable even to speak.

That day in Thailand changed my life. I was in the best shape of my life. Competing in and finishing the biggest race of my life was a long-term goal of mine, and as I was heading home I was exhausted but exhilarated. Leading up to that race, I had been going non-stop—overworking, training, traveling, developing professionally, socializing, networking. All the things, all at once. I'd been going full throttle and not listening fully to my body. I had been consistently pushing myself past my own limits. I wasn't taking those pauses or moments to slow down and recharge. So, as life often does, it hands us moments that force us to slow down.

This accident was an abrupt reset for me, one that I wouldn't wish on anyone. I found myself in these moments of slow recovery where my brain just didn't work like it used to, where I didn't feel like myself anymore, and where I constantly questioned whether I was being a burden to those that I love. Those were some of the hardest moments I've ever had to endure. That feeling of being a burden was one that took me down a spiral, a dark spiral, where I found myself having suicidal thoughts because I didn't want to be this version of me.

Over time I learned that our mind plays tricks on us and that our brain is like a muscle. It can be rebuilt. That being said, I wasn't quite ready for the rebuilding part of my recovery. I needed to go within and to feel sorry for myself for a while. Experiencing something traumatic requires a time to grieve what we lost and will be losing and to fully feel into what happened.

Fortunately, I have always been someone who rebounds quickly. I am certain this stems from my sports career and experiences. When we fall or get boarded in hockey, we get back up and skate harder, when we fall on our bike, we jump back on and peddle faster. When we finish a game, even after being stomped on in a scrum, we power through injuries until the game is over. This has proven to me that our brains can push through and cross any literal or metaphorical finish line. Reminding myself of this, is now almost second nature. No matter what I'm facing, I know there is light at the end of every dark tunnel.

Even with my experience in sports, athletic achievements and mind-over-matter outlook, at that moment, sitting in the hospital in Thailand and then when bedridden upon my return home, I needed to come into this place where I truly understood what was happening and to truly understand the brain and the injury I had received. So, I had neuropsychologists, neurosurgeons, friends, family, educators, and psychologists come to me with the information about brain injuries so I could understand what was happening to me. I had never experienced anything like this before and decided the next step was to try and make sense of the situation.

As I began to learn more and more about my brain injury and how to rebuild after my experience, I started to write motivational quotes and words all over my mirrors in erasable markers. I had a large whiteboard on the wall in a place I knew I would see every morning, and wrote out my new goals and aspirations. I set short term and long-term goals, and wrote down all the things that I needed to accomplish to be able to reach that end goal. This made things very clear for me. I hired the most incredible coach, Ken Hamilton, who started my recovery training with just ten minutes a day. We then moved to twenty, thirty, then eventually forty, and so on. He helped me get back on track and prepared my body and mind for the next best version of me.

From a newfound place of self-acceptance and understanding, I was able to make some decisions. I realized that I had been presented with the opportunity before my accident and while preparing for that last Ironman, to compete for Team Canada in my age group (30-35) for a sprint at the ITU World Triathlon Final in London, England. This is a world-wide event where athletes compete for a position. After the accident, I did not think this was even a possibility anymore. At first, I could not string full sentences together, I could not write an email, I broke all my ribs and if you have ever had a broken rib, you know the pain. I forgot memories and people, I lost feeling in my right arm, I had multiple stitches in my head and face. I was a mess and swirling into a place with the darkest thoughts I had ever had. I questioned if I would ever race again, if my memories would return, if my words and years of education would ever come back, if my family and friends would still love me. These thoughts were terrifying—and spiraling.

I don't remember the exact moment that brought me to this place of conviction. I eventually came to the point where I decided that I'm doing it anyway. "Fuck it. I'm going to figure out a way because I always do." But, my recovery was slow because there was not only the mental damage but the physical damage to my body that I had to move through. I had to honor this time of healing. I remember thinking even if I come in last place, it is important for me to dream again. To have a dream that I can go after, that I can work towards, one that I can visualize as I lay here recovering. I envisioned myself crossing that finish line, feeling the exhilaration of doing something that I didn't know I would be able to do.

I didn't care what place I finished in, this new dream and aspiration was simply about competing and finishing. It was about remembering what it felt like to achieve beyond what was possible. It was about setting a new goal and meeting it. I was reframing what competition meant for me. It was no longer about who came in first or last, it became about being the best version of myself at whatever stage of life or recovery I was in.

These moments of doing something primarily to be the best version of myself are what I call *finish line experiences*. Whether it's climbing to the top of a mountain, walking across that stage to get my degree, or literally running across a finish line in a race, each one has taught me something about discipline, achievement, and focusing on my next best. That's why I live by this ***reset, realize, reframe, and recommit*** mindset each day, and teach to others through my work.

When an unexpected event happens, I remind myself to see it as a reset—it's not the end of the road. I take time to reflect and realize what's actually going on. This often means talking to trusted friends, seeking help from professionals, asking questions, reading, or learning as much as I can about the situation. Eventually, I gain clarity and start to see where I am. That's when I can begin to reframe my new path, which is such an exciting step. It's like standing in front of a blank canvas, with all the colors, glitter, gems, and anything else I want to create my own masterpiece. That frame is mine to design, adjust, and shape however I want. It's all about building the mental muscle to bring myself to a place of *resetting, realizing, reframing, and recommitting* to a dream—even if it's a brand new one.

My original dream was to win gold for Team Canada. What I ended up fighting for was the finish line and I crossed it. Reframing is not settling. I crossed that finish line with goosebumps the size of golf balls and a waterfall of tears of joy. What I accomplished was so much more meaningful and rewarding. Getting up again, not giving up, and crossing that finish line was so much bigger and so much more important than anything I could have dreamt of before. And I am not done. I've proven to myself that I can overcome the challenges and obstacles in front of me and now my dreams can be bigger than ever.

So, if you have forgotten your dream, or you have gotten sidetracked, or you have faced a big reset moment (hopefully without involving a windshield and a concrete wall), or a big challenge or moment in your life where things have gone sideways, get curious with how you can realize, reframe, and then recommit to your dream. Because recommitting to your dreams will drive you to that next greatest version of you. And you will love it.

"In the middle of every difficulty lies opportunity."
—Albert Einstein

Erica Bearss

Erica Bearss first pursued excellence in sport, winning two gold medals in Ontario provincial ringette, playing varsity field hockey, AAA ice hockey for BC, and competing for Team Canada at the ITU World Triathlon Grand Final in London, England. Alongside her athletic career, Erica advocates for education. She completed a BA with Honors in Modern Languages and Literature, an MBA in Leadership and Management, and after years of industry experience, now teaches at universities and technical colleges across North America. Erica has held several leadership and consulting roles in a variety of industries. She also has a passion for acting. Her participation in community theater complements regular appearances on stage, in commercials, and short films.

A natural adventurer and leader, Erica is an avid traveler fluent in English, French, and Spanish. Most importantly, Erica is a dedicated mother of two bright and inspiring young boys who are already developing into athletes and adventurers themselves. Together, they continue to seek new challenges and discover new opportunities. Erica lives and works with a mindset of collaboration, innovation, and excellence. Connect or PM me on LinkedIn www.linkedin.com/in/ericabearssmba Or check out my LinkTree: https://linktr.ee/ericabearss.

My logical brain knew that I was not in danger, but my nervous system was preparing to fight for my life.

CHAPTER 12

Healthcare Human

Paige Mathison

In a moment, the ability to maintain my composure vanished, and my entire sense of self was challenged. I'd been a psychiatric nurse for over a decade when I was struck with symptoms of Post-Traumatic Stress Disorder. After an extensive and erratic patient interaction, it felt like a switch in my brain went from online to broken in an instant.

A Nurse Is Born

For most of my adult life, I thought I was lucky to know what I wanted to be when I grew up. In grade nine, I declared my plan to become a psychiatric nurse after a rebellious middle school experience. Some friends at the time shared their time in psychiatric facilities, and I was thrilled to learn that I did not need to become a physician to support mental health. From there, I began dedicating my energy to bringing that goal to fruition.

As early as I was twelve, I remember my caregiving nature creating safety for others to be open and share their hurts. I found great joy in conversation, learning about mental health, and having visions of being "the cool nurse," who made compassionate connections and advocated for her suffering patients.

I believe we all have innate gifts that we bring into the world. At some point, our gifts are asked to be packaged, labeled, and then placed into a socially acceptable box. Strengths are turned into something monetizable and, with hope, contribute to the greater good.

Once I completed high school, my life revolved around checking the educational boxes required to reach the career I felt so passionate about. I was fired up to be part of a community with the same goals as I did in supporting others.

The intention I set was achievable, but only to a certain degree. Nothing can truly prepare anyone for the realities and responsibilities of their roles, until they have been fully immersed in the scarcity that exists within many healthcare settings. Those limitations wear on our passions and create holes in our protective shields meant to guard us against becoming traumatized.

Looking back to my pre-nursing years, while I was finding worth in holding space for youth in pain, a seed had been planted and was growing into a sense of identity. Throughout my education and time as a nurse, it continued to be fertilized by a belief system that self-sacrifice was noble, and anything less was undutiful. Because the soil was within me, these ideologies bled into my personal life, not realizing how deeply rooted my attachment to being a caregiver. It eventually became my way of feeling a sense of belonging...

A sense of belonging that, when unexpectedly shattered, created an inner turmoil that I wish upon no one.

When My Body Said "No More"

During a shift that felt no different than any other, one of my patients was in distress. As always, I immediately went into action to attempt to alleviate their discomfort and provide a sense of relief. Regardless of the steps I took, I was verbally and psychologically abused for hours.

This is not an unusual scenario for many healthcare providers and is more common than many know. As caregivers, we often have the ability to separate the person from their reactions, knowing that upset can induce actions that cause harm. For some reason, though, my brain could no longer intellectualize the hurtful words, and my survival instinct of "make it stop" kicked in.

It took everything in my power to stifle the response my body was craving in that moment. Although I know I would never want to hurt anyone, every cell felt like it was screaming to protect me. I remember a sensation in my throat as though I was literally swallowing the guttural impulse to match their volume and create space from the attack.

In an instant, darkness washed over me as though every trauma throughout my lifetime came rising to the surface. Every moment of hurt, grief, struggle, and abuse that devastated my vulnerable heart was exposed. And in that moment, I thought, "I am not okay..." but tried to push it down, which I'd become more than accustomed to doing.

My body had other plans. After safely settling the situation and heading into the nursing station, tears started to flow, and my body vibrated. Panic started rising with thoughts that my expression was unsafe for anyone to see. It felt wrong to share this emotional release, and I experienced fear that I would be regarded as weak.

I was in a trauma response, and my emotions refused to be kept inside any longer. My colleagues looked at me with confusion, as they had known me as someone who minimally wavered in times of crisis. The most prominent emotions? Rage and fear sat on the surface, begging for acknowledgment.

No one ever anticipates that their worldview will be changed forever. And until you've experienced it, you don't realize how uncomfortable your thoughts can be. I'd experienced depression and anxiety, plus been through substantial losses, but suddenly my trust in my ability to cope had vanished. I learned that it is possible to experience nearly inconsolable fear and anger while feeling unsure of how I will carry on living.

At that time, it felt like it was okay for others to have meltdowns, but I quickly realized that the level of safety may not be the same for me. The standard was different for me because I should know what to do. I needed to be relied upon by my colleagues and could not measure up to what I held myself to. One common inner critic would say, "You are a mental health professional and you can't even take care of your own." A worry-based one was, "My brain feels broken. Will it be like this forever?"

I craved understanding more than ever in times of such deep shame and disbelief. I could barely leave my home without spiraling into an anxiety-based narrative. A few hours of emotional torture during that overwhelming shift resulted in intensive trauma therapy for ten months and not being able to work.

This created so much additional shame, and it took me to a dark place where healing felt nearly impossible. I was no longer at work, yet I felt I needed to uphold a certain persona. I'd been diagnosed with a workplace mental health injury but was afraid to say anything to my colleagues. Would they understand? I hadn't heard of others being off work due to being yelled at, so why wouldn't I think I was the anomaly? So I tried to be light-hearted about it, make jokes, and minimize just how agonizing each day could be.

As with any person, it can be life-changing to safely work through our wounds so that we can experience the world without viewing it through a lens of our past traumas. That said, it is an incredibly vulnerable journey. At the time, I felt broken and worried I would never be able to return to supporting those suffering. The guilt associated with not being on the frontlines during the beginning phases of the pandemic also consumed me.

My nervous system was so overstimulated that I couldn't even watch an online video about psychiatric units without going into a state of crisis. Yet, there I was, beating myself up for not being able to suck it up and do my job. My logical brain knew that I was not in danger, but my nervous system was preparing to fight for my life. I felt utterly conflicted between one part of me wanting to uphold my duty as a nurse while the other side desperately wanted me to avoid anything that reminded me of the hospital.

Thankfully, I completed the proper steps, which led me to the path of recovery, but not without countless moments of judgment and the minimizing of my experience. Yes, I was being hard on myself, but there were a multitude of misguided comments from others. One response included criticism of my decision to refuse unsafe work during that trauma-inducing shift and many more questions of, "Why don't you just go back to work?" surfaced.

After many hours of Exposure Therapy and Eye Movement Desensitization and Reprocessing, I returned to the very same unit where I experienced the incident. Looking back, I realize I never entirely removed the professional mask when in sessions and still need to be conscious of this when seeking support. Not only from a vulnerability viewpoint, it is also hard to switch places from the person helping to the person being helped.

Even so, my time re-storying the traumatizing shift and returning my nervous system nearly back to baseline, I felt ready to return to work. Although I was going back to where I'd been many times before, it was with new perspectives.

One of the most profound lessons I experienced during my healing journey was a greater need for compassion, not just for others, but most of all for myself. While I was acknowledging the humanness of my patients, I was not providing the same level of grace to those working beside me. By going through my struggles, I learned that managing our responsibilities during a shift is possible while also receiving kindness in our errors and biological responses to stress.

A collective is a community, and the encouragement around teamwork in the healthcare system could be more reflective of this. I can imagine a space that feels genuinely empowering and supportive, focusing on safely accepting accountability rather than inducing a fear of failure and the threat of being exiled for not living up to unreasonable expectations.

Intense work conditions had become completely normalized in my life, so after stepping back, I wasn't as blind to the amount of responsibility held in the hands of healthcare providers and first responders. We have the lived experience carrying the knowledge and skills to provide competent care. Still, one key factor in reducing the chances of becoming traumatized is knowing that we'll be accepted if we flounder.

I also reflected on what it means to be truly trauma-informed and recognized the format can be used among each other as caregivers. After better understanding the language around survival responses and having first-hand experience with the social, mental, physical, and spiritual impacts, I could truly acknowledge that it can happen to anyone without knowing what may trigger it. Because we have many similar experiences when working in the same environment, who would be better than each other to offer compassionate support?

When in a state of overwhelm, our critical thinking ability inevitably decreases because we are in survival mode. This is one of the reasons why those in the helping fields complete intensive training and are required to continue learning to ensure we know the processes and procedures to support during tragic circumstances. We go into professional mode and hope to come out on the other side with successful outcomes. So often, there are losses instead of wins, and we do not have an opportunity to process them before heading into the next situation.

If I'd been able to label that I had been traumatized without feeling like an inferior nurse, maybe my time away from the hospital would have been shorter. I'd argue that my biggest obstacle in my recovery was beating myself up for not being able to make it through an abusive situation unscathed. Normalizing my response would have felt much better than internally and externally repeating, "I didn't even get hit..." countless times after that shift. I know of others who felt the same, but I did not get to choose my last straw scenario, nor do I think anyone gets that opportunity.

I dream of a system that is so well-resourced that if, after an incident occurs and someone's nervous system interprets it as too much to handle, they can safely step away to nourish themselves. That each person could catch the activated state of the body and, without shame, provide comfort through their senses, presence, or paid time off to allow the stress hormones to reduce.

Personally, I never want to hit a point of debilitating anguish before I attend to my needs, but I know this is a widespread occurrence. Even when in disabling mental pain, I still felt that pressure to return to work and that I was letting others down. Still today, I catch myself listening to those inner messages, but know I am creating more space for my humanness each day.

When challenges arise, I now have a deep knowing that there is an opportunity for post-traumatic growth. Through understanding, genuine support, lessening the intensity of the pain, and learning ways to move forward, I am building my capacity to navigate change.

Now, as a clinical counselor, public speaker, and group mental health practice owner, I strive to inject compassion into whatever settings I possibly can, like I always imagined I would do when I was young and only envisioning my life as a nurse. Better yet, I am confident in knowing how much I value my time supporting others and that I can provide an individualized touch to my work. Yes, I have a professional title, but the care I provide is the mark I leave on the world, not the licensing.

Each of us is unique and beautiful, yet when we choose any career, I now realize that we also choose blanket expectations from others. Assumptions become ingrained as honorable while others are barely acknowledged, even though everyone's roles have meaning. We all navigate biases and unsolicited opinions regarding what we do, especially when in the eyes of the public.

It can be a defining moment when you are ultimately transitioning into your new career. It's like that decision defines us in some way. I remember near the end of my undergraduate program a professor commented something along the lines of no longer having the privilege of a mental illness because we were soon to be nurses. This message was internalized in a way that created unrealistic viewpoints and judgments, as many in the healthcare field know all too well.

Here's the thing, though, we are trauma-exposed professionals who often are the people encountered during the worst periods of others lives. Healthcare workers, police, fire, emergency medical services, and many more humans walk alongside those experiencing grief or horrific events and seek comfort from those who know how to respond.

And that is our choice. We have chosen to do this because many of us have a deep sense of wanting to make a difference, connect, see someone, and hold space for them in their pain. Providing compassionate understanding and quality care is a privilege, especially when able to bring any amount of peace into chaos and for those feeling broken.

That said, I am compelled to soften the stigma that still exists around mental health crises and not only for those in society asking for help. It is also essential to acknowledge the humanness of those trained to repress parts of themselves for the sake of a stoic persona often needed during a crisis. These are the people problem-solving treatment for illness, giving CPR to someone who has lost a pulse, actively in the line of violence, making life-or-death choices, and listening to the screams of people amid loss. Those who often are not acknowledged beyond the uniform to the human wearing it.

When considering the word hero, as was often used during the pandemic for healthcare workers, I think of the words from Romain Rolland, "A hero is a man who does what he can." As I mentioned previously, we all hold special gifts that can be used toward the greater good. Most helping professionals intend to do everything they can to protect those they serve.

Each of us could use more compassion provided to us. We all have experienced some form of adversity, and if not yet, we know there will come a time. No one is immune to struggle, as I have sat and listened to countless stories from those who have given me the honor of hearing them.

Integrating the Meaning

Instead of the professor's perception of healthcare providers no longer having the capability to experience struggles with their own mental health, with great appreciation, I'd welcome another conversation. Dialogue around the reality that being exposed to trauma nearly daily can make it incredibly difficult to clock out after clocking in.

Characters from comic books have a version of Kryptonite, so why can't we consider that humans need more nurturing and understanding? As people working in heroic roles, whether you choose to see the sacrifices they make or not, they each have limitations. Limitations are what make us human, which is why the pedestals that anyone gets placed on or pushed off should be at reasonable heights.

The potential to experience a mental health injury lingers for any trauma-exposed professional in every industry. I choose to honor that truth and have been dedicating my life to enhancing the availability of connection and empowerment for caregivers in crisis. Although only in the beginning phases of this journey, I am provoking ripples that are slowly growing toward waves. Even sharing my story here can potentially add to creating a non-judgemental space where those we call heroes can safely be heard and feel seen.

Could we honor this reality together? Things could be substantially different for those riddled with shame after not living up to the often high expectations of their career or environment. Could we consider some pause before judgment and inject a little more humanity into our interactions? I'd love to experience a world with growing compassion so that we do not need to expel so much energy combating stigma and be able to save our strength for getting through difficult times or supporting others through theirs.

PAIGE MATHISON

Paige Mathison is a clinical counselor specializing in trauma care and the founder of Another Chapter Counselling, based in British Columbia. Her lived experience as a trauma-survivor and psychiatric nurse enhances her therapeutic approach, especially for those who are working in the healthcare field.

She also loves demystify complex topics with humor as a public speaker after years of being a stand-up comedian. Paige often speaks on topics such as burnout, enhancing joy, the power of laughter and building a trauma-informed lens. Her love of adventure is re-sparking after many years of dedicated energy toward her business, and looking forward to more travel, presence and fun!

Website: www.paigemathison.com
Email: paigemathisonspeaks@gmail.com
Instagram: @detraumatizinghealthcare
TikTok: @detraumatizinghealthcare

The journey from darkness to light is not an easy one, but it is one worth taking.

Silent Echoes

Dhorea Ramanula

The gun went off, his body fell into the fetal position, and the rise of gun smoke left his body at the same time as his breath. I paused and then this massive guttural scream rose out of me from such a deep and foreign place that I didn't recognize the sound. A minute before I'd been talking to the love of my life, and the next minute he was on the floor dead. I froze, and in that moment my whole life changed. Witnessing someone leaving this Earth, someone you love so much—is mind-numbing.

I was in shock and I didn't know what to do, so I called my mom, "Kevin's dead!" I screamed.

"I can't wake him up. Please help me, Momma. Please! I don't know what to do." Then all I remember is that I was screaming and crying and pacing and losing my mind. I don't even remember hanging up the phone or walking to the closet. But, the next thing I knew, the SWAT team and police were at my penthouse apartment opening the closet door because I was still hidden there, unable to know where to go or what to do. I'm pretty sure they could see that there was no one in my body.

Later as I sat at the police station explaining what happened, I still felt dazed. And of course, because they knew I had nothing to do with it, they let me go. One of the hardest parts of the entire experience was finding out the way he had shot the gun. Being an award winning dental surgeon, he had shot himself with such precision that it went right through his brain with very little blood. It also went through the high back of my chair, and had I been a few inches over, I would be lying right beside him. The news was too much for my body and brain to comprehend. My soul couldn't take it. All I remember is that when I left the police department it was beautiful and sunny out, and I walked all the way home. How I got there, I can't say. I was lost and alone. All I know is that my life forever changed on that day.

Even so, the brutal reality is that the death of my husband wasn't my first experience with suicide nor was it my last. The first time I witnessed suicide, and the huge and massive domino effect it leaves on all of those left behind, was when I was eighteen. At that time, I lived with this wonderful artist. He was amazing, eclectic, and brilliant. I was young and bright and full of life. Things felt amazing. Then one day I came home and there was a note written on our loft wall stating that he'd had to leave this life and leave me. When I looked up, he was hanging there by a rafter. I wish I could have saved him but I couldn't and neither could the paramedics.

That day is forever cemented in my mind. The reason I felt I was able to heal and build a life after this was that his parents and the community rallied around me. We grieved and healed from a true place and I was not isolated or shunned. My life, I thought, had had some very real and heavy trauma and like any resilient woman I went on to do my career and put my head down. I believed that because of this horrible experience and accepting how I truly changed from it, my life now would be easy, or at least easier. I was terribly wrong, but at such a young age, what did I truly know? How can anyone predict that this could possibly happen to one human twice in a lifetime.

Trauma in isolation hijacks your brain, and shadows over your soul. And at only twenty-seven years old, it felt like I was carrying the weight of the world on my shoulders. So, on the first of May, two years to the anniversary of the death of my husband, I found myself in such a deep and dark space. I was desperately trying to understand why I couldn't shake the feeling of not being enough, of low self-esteem, low self-confidence, and such vast emptiness. I didn't want to die but I couldn't accept this as life. All I wanted was for the pain to go away and the constant darkness in my soul to be lightened—to be less. So I went to a restaurant, swallowed 182 pills, then I drove to see my mom, said how much I loved her, that I was sorry, and said goodbye.

Three days later I woke up in the hospital with all of these wires attached to me, monitoring my heart and other vitals. What really stuck with me though, was the horror on my mom's face and the look in her eyes. I could see a sorrow so deeply massive, that when I came to, I vowed to make what I could of my life as a deep apology to her. The fact that I survived also prompted me to vow to commit my life to service and suicide prevention. Lying there in that hospital bed, I didn't know how I was going to do it, but I knew I had to.

Ultimately, that hospital room became the catalyst for my journey to becoming a pillar of strength for others. Following my suicide attempt, I embarked on a profound journey of healing and self-discovery. This was not easy, nor was it short. After the three-day coma, I spent several months on the psych ward so I wouldn't harm myself. During that time, they did massive rapid eye movement therapy. It was back in the nineties when it was still new, and I went on this long healing journey of therapy and the deep-rootedness of why I didn't feel like I was enough. I answered hard questions for myself like: "Why did I feel that I needed to leave this Earth?" "Why did I attract people into my life that wanted to leave me?" It was such a long and painful and gut-wrenching journey of self-discovery, but I did it.

At the heart of the process was uncovering the journey of my life and the role that had played on who I was. You see, I grew up in chaos and crisis. I had a wonderful mom who had me at seventeen and decided to keep me. Which, looking back I think was terribly brave of her, but she came with her own demons in her life history. And, shortly after I was born, she fell heavily into addiction—alcoholism.

Life with my mother, Hemi, was full of excitement, and crazy-making. She danced with the Royal Winnipeg Ballet, and we traveled together from a very young age, surrounded by eclectic folks and always living on the fringe of very wealthy and influential people. What a dichotomy—rising from poverty, at the tender age of innocence, I stepped into conditioning to ensure we presented well, to the highest standard of existence.

My childhood was a constant ping pong game between excitement and chaos. Because of that, I had so many traumatic things that happened to me throughout my lifetime. Like the time I was seven years old and she forgot that I was coming home. When I got there, the door was locked and so I slept on the porch. That night our house burned down while she was inside. She made it out alive. But, moments like that played on my self-esteem, my self-worth, and my self-confidence. I am Métis and Black-and-white and have never quite known where to fit in. All of this layered my experience, and the societal expectation to present a perfect image was a significant challenge for me.

Growing up with a mother who battled addiction meant that I was always aware of how we were perceived by others. The pressure to appear flawless and untroubled was immense, and it left little room for genuine self-expression. I became adept at hiding my true feelings, masking my pain with a façade of composure.

Therefore, during the time that followed my suicide attempt, I began to lean into my pain from childhood and all its uncomfortableness. I learned to ask for help. I found my tribe. I spoke my truth, giving power and voice to the sweet little girl inside me screaming to share that I am here. I am worthy. Please see me, understand me, validate me. Through the process, I quickly realized I needed to do all of these things for myself first. I built trust inside my body, mind, and soul, then the world started to mirror me.

Ultimately, my journey to healing began with embracing vulnerability. I had to acknowledge my pain and allow myself to feel it fully. This was a daunting process, as it required dismantling the walls I had built around my heart. But it was a necessary step toward genuine healing. So, I sought therapy and joined support groups where I could share my experiences without fear of judgment. These spaces provided a sense of belonging and validation that I had longed for. I realized that I was not alone in my struggles and that there were others who understood my pain.

This period of healing in my life is what I, and many others, call the dark night of the soul. And on many levels it was a deeply cathartic experience that led me to create the documentary on suicide warning signs and co-founding initiatives like National Suicide Awareness Day. My academic contributions, including research published in the Journal of Dental Education, focused on understanding the factors contributing to suicide among dentists.

All of my efforts were to find meaning in my pain—to use my pain to prevent others from experiencing the same. It was also about taking that deep-rooted pain hiding inside me and sharing it in a safe space, giving others space to share and heal as well. I toured and spoke to high school students, the community, firefighters, healthcare professionals, anyone who would listen. This became a mission greater than my own existence. It was tumultuous at times. I was battling the school system and others that thought if you speak about suicide and prevention people will do it, BUT what law makers and policy issuers do not understand is that suicide breeds in isolation. It makes you think this is the only way out and it is not. With support you can live through it, and so I had to convince people that speaking about the suicide was more likely to prevent people from choosing it. Educating folks on the warning signs gives you hope that you can pay attention and then get help. It puts the power back in their hands and in those that love them and know how serious this issue is and how preventable it is. But we must first have awareness.

Now every day I decide to live my life in a way that is human-centered and to be a person of service. I get to help people uncover that they are not alone and that they are worthy simply by breathing. Because of this human-centric approach each day, I've been able to help support over 10,000 people in choosing life and provide individuals with a safe space to be seen, heard, and find their truth without judgment.

As I look back on my journey, I see a tapestry woven with the threads of pain and resilience, despair and hope, loss and love. Each thread tells a story, and together they form a narrative that is uniquely mine yet universally relatable. The journey from darkness to light is not an easy one, but it is one worth taking. As I continue to walk this path, I carry with me the stories of those I have touched and those who have touched me, each one a reminder that we are never truly alone.

Today, I am an amazing community member who is about to open up a holistic healing center which is a space for women in recovery. It's called Hemi's House, inspired by my mother, Hemi, who did eventually get sober. It's a holistic, wrap-around support approach to recovery to help women thrive. It's my life's work and I feel so honored and so moved to be able to do this every day.

Choosing life is not a one-time decision but a continuous commitment to oneself, to hold space, and touch the hearts of those around us. My work isn't just about my career or achievements; it's about the innate need to connect, to gift words of hope, and to inspire change. To end living in isolation, pain, or a lack of self-compassion and empathy for the journey others have walked, because when we open our hearts and align our minds while living in the truest essence of our spirit, we will rise because there is no community without unity.

Dhorea is writing a book of poems exploring her life experiences. You can find one of her poems, The Dark Night of the Soul, in the Appendix at the back of this book.

DHOREA RAMANULA

Dhorea Ramanula is a multifaceted leader and advocate, renowned for her co-founding of National Suicide Awareness Day. She has been published in the Journal of Dental Education and produced an award-winning documentary on healthy living. Dhorea serves as Board Chair, President, and Community Engagement Facilitator at the Faculty of Management at University of British Columbia Okanagan. As the only Canadian featured in Times Square, New York, for International Women's Day, she is a beacon of inspiration. In 2024, she received an Honorable Mention for the Women of the Year/Spirit Award with Kelowna Women in Business. Dhorea founded Hemi's Holistic Healing Centre Society, championing inclusive holistic recovery for women. Her unwavering commitment to mental health, education, and community empowerment has made her a respected and influential figure in her field. You can find Dhorea on the socials at @Dhorea08 and you can email her directly at hemiholistic@gmaill.com and info@hemishealingcentre.com.

I still have days when I question who I am.

Sensitivity Advisory:
This chapter references personal experiences of bullying.

CHAPTER 14

Finding Home: The Journey of Discovering Identity and Belonging

Ania Trimble

Most of my life I looked to others for confirmation of who I was. Always looking outside of myself for love, approval, belonging, and acceptance. It felt like I was desperately searching for my identity in all the labels society creates for us, and somewhere along the way I lost touch of who I really was.

Growing up I moved from country to country and as a result, no place truly ever felt like home. The first time we moved was when I was seven and we left Poland. My father was not able to accompany us at the time, so it was just the three of us—my mom, my sister, and I.

This first year in Germany was challenging; I constantly felt like I had to find my place and build new friendships, while also missing my dad. Throughout this time, my dad and I exchanged letters and phone calls, but it was not the same. I missed him dearly. My dad and I had always had a special bond. It felt like we were two peas in a pod. We understood one another on a level my mother and I did not. Leaving Poland without him created a feeling of insecurity and a lack of safety for me. There was a piece of me that never felt fully supported when we were apart.

When we were finally reunited as a family, it brought a sense of gratitude and completion to our family unit. My sense of safety and belonging also returned to some degree. Still, despite the initial joy of our reunion, readjusting to his presence in our lives required a period of adaptation and acclimatization for all of us.

So much so, that one day, my mother left with my sister while my father was at work. Initially, she mentioned that they were going shopping. But, they did not return by the time my father arrived home and for a long time after that. This unexpected turn of events left me bewildered and uncertain about the situation between my parents.

Eventually my mother and sister did return. But, like many childhood memories that we bury or suppress, the duration of my mother's absence remains a mystery. Whether it spanned hours, days, or even a week—I don't know. This episode became a buried memory that was never openly addressed or discussed. All I know is that the trauma of this event significantly influenced my life, leading to occasional struggles, particularly concerning self-esteem and trust in others.

The displacement I felt in childhood continued, and at the age of ten, one year away from being a citizen of Germany, my entire family had to move to Canada. It was 1989, the year the Berlin Wall came down finally reuniting East and West Germany. This meant that anyone who was not a citizen of Germany had to choose to return to their homeland, or apply to live in another country that was willing to accept immigrants.

Adjusting to a new country for the second time in my life and grappling with another foreign language introduced many new hurdles in my quest for a sense of belonging. Struggling with language barriers, I endured bullying throughout elementary and junior high school due to my appearance and weight. Lacking the slender legs that were idealized, I was subjected to hurtful taunts about my legs being likened to "tree trunks." And during moments of vulnerability, I found myself the target of spitballs while silently praying for acceptance and inclusion. I longed to be chosen as a valued team member, to be embraced by peers, and to feel a sense of belonging. Questions plagued my mind about what made me unworthy of friendship in their eyes.

Eventually, I chose to change schools after finishing junior high and decided to venture out to a different high school than the rest of my classmates. In taking this step, I chose to begin a new journey because I was able to change my environment and start fresh. This step helped me see that I had the power to show the world that I am capable of being who I want to be and no one can tell me otherwise. It's also the step that pushed me to become passionate about health and nutrition, which is ultimately how I learned to gain confidence in myself.

Still, despite the confidence I gained, my struggles with identity continued into adulthood. And, becoming a mother marked another significant moment where I struggled with my identity and underwent a transformation. Prior to welcoming my daughter, my priorities centered around personal fitness, with a regimen of five to six workouts weekly, a commitment to healthy eating, and a career as a nurse. Despite the profound body changes that motherhood brought, I was determined to reclaim my pre-baby routine, but this proved to be challenging. It wasn't just me any longer. There were two of us now, and in addition to adjusting to the tasks of mothering, I had to discover who I was as a mother. I had to be more structured and intentional in modifying my pre-baby routine to fit my new life and schedule so that I didn't lose my passion for health and nutrition during this new time of transition. I was determined to maintain the identity that I'd worked so hard to create for myself during young adulthood.

Then, six years later my world came to a profound halt when my dad was diagnosed with stage four pancreatic cancer. As a nurse I understood the gravity of this situation, foreseeing the inevitable outcome and feeling the loss and grief before he even passed. His journey through his illness created turbulence in my life and relationships. There were many dark and lonely days. I eventually learned that I needed to accept that things were beyond my control or I was going to be buried in my grief and face losing myself to the loss of my father and what our close relationship meant to my life.

For me, loving and honoring myself and my identity is an ongoing journey that I work on daily. I've learned that setting boundaries is not always easy, and I've lost friendships and struggled with relationships at times. Putting myself first does not mean being selfish, it means doing the work even when I really don't want to, facing difficult conversations with myself and others. It means creating a life with meaning and not letting life just pass me by. As I get older I value different things like my physical and mental health above all and giving myself the space and grace is an important part of my wellbeing. I still have days when I question who I am. I still have days when I lack confidence. I still have days where the juggling of motherhood and career is hard. But I am learning, and growing; self-healing is a lifelong journey.

And, through life's many challenges and experiences I have learned that it was no longer important to put my energy in the past as it was not serving me. In my lifetime I may never get the answers I want to questions about why my mom and sister left and why I was left behind, or why I was not the popular girl in class. But, I know these experiences have shaped me into who I am today. And, by continuing to put in the work and giving myself grace when needed, I can recognize and accept that it's not going to be easy, but it will be worth it. I am not perfect. I come with my flaws and shitty parts but they make me who I am today and make me more aware of who I still want to be; a woman who takes charge of her life, who decides her own identity, and a mother that gives it her best everyday.

To this day I have a diary that is holding all the dark moments of shame, humiliation, fear, and the deep desire to belong that has been woven throughout my life. This diary is full of writings where I put pen to paper, and expressed my fears, my rage, hurt, grief, and my sadness and anger of being alone in it all. This diary lives somewhere deep in my closet with the hidden stories and experiences of my youth. There are times when I find myself looking at this diary. It's pink, pretty, and shiny on the outside full of pages of darkness on the inside. Stories and experiences that no one else knows about but me. I lost the key years ago. And, at times I'm tempted to just bust it open and revisit my journey, and see how far I've come. Other times I just want to toss it in the trash. For some reason though, I keep it and put it back in my closet far enough to forget and find it again by mistake. To me it's a reminder that so many of us walk through life feeling alone. My hope is that through reading my journey you'll feel less alone in your own struggles whatever those may be.

ANIA TRIMBLE

Ania Trimble is a devoted nurse with sixteen years of experience, with a profound commitment to holistic health. Additionally, she serves as a holistic nutritional weight loss and hormone coach while balancing her role as a mother to her twelve-year-old daughter. Beyond her family commitments, Anna dedicates her time to empowering clients to regain equilibrium and vitality. Through her guidance, she encourages clients to embrace lifestyle modifications that nourish their bodies from the inside out. Get to know Anna on Instagram at @balanceholisticnutrition.yeg.

I didn't comprehend the long-term impact the decision to stuff my feelings down would have on my life.

CHAPTER 15

The Power Within: My Path to Reclaiming Strength and Purpose

Anita Parker

During a session with an energy healer, she moved her hands over my body, stopping above my abdomen, and asked if there was a piece of me that was dead. Instantly, I knew she was referring to my seventeen-year-old self—the part of me that I'd judged so harshly for almost thirty years.

Leading up to that moment, I'd done so much great healing in other areas of my life. I'd healed generational trauma from sexual abuse. I'd overcome the aftermath of divorce. But the shame and judgment I felt for a decision I'd made at seventeen was one area in my life where I was stuck. And, as a successful entrepreneur on the cusp of big things, I knew that I needed to revisit, retrieve, and heal it in order to fully step into my power.

Because, despite all the healing I had done, there was still this one part of my past that I had never fully confronted. That choice I made at seventeen, buried under layers of shame and judgment, was still holding me back. I knew I couldn't move forward, couldn't step into the woman I was becoming, without facing it head-on.

At seventeen, I was dating my high school sweetheart and was in a party phase, using alcohol and drugs to mask the pain from childhood abuse. And, although I was a social butterfly, I felt utterly alone. The abandonment by my father was more challenging to navigate than I'd realized. My mother, busy working multiple jobs to support us, left me to find my way through the complexities of my experience, often leading me to self-soothe in unhealthy ways.

When my highschool sweetheart and I unexpectedly became

pregnant, I was scared. I didn't know what to do and we chose to end the pregnancy. Immediately after having the abortion, despite thoughts of being a murderer, I remember thinking, *"No. I don't need this feeling,"* I wanted to hit the delete button on having to think about it. As if my body couldn't handle carrying the pain and shame I felt without looking at it and processing it. So I just didn't think about it. Ever. And, at seventeen, I didn't comprehend the long-term impact the decision to stuff my feelings down would have on my life—and the shame and judgment I would carry for that seventeen year old version of myself for decades as a result.

The path to self-forgiveness wasn't easy nor was it straightforward for me. However, it's played such a crucial role in my healing journey. Forgiving myself for the choices I made and the pain I'd carried was a pivotal step towards reclaiming my wholeness and fully stepping into my calling to bring community and people together. I was fortunate to have a supportive network of individuals who guided and encouraged me through the process. Which involved a lot of journaling and visualization where I'd pictured myself wrapping that sweet seventeen year old version of myself in a hug and showering her with love and forgiveness.

It also involved looking at the feelings and judgment towards my seventeen year old self for the first time, rather than trying to hit the delete button on the files in my brain. When I did that, I started to see just how much of my life had been affected by stuffing my feelings down.

One of the biggest areas I realized it showed up was in my relationship with my daughter who I had at thirty. When she reached seventeen, I felt an inexplicable pull back from her. And, upon deeper reflection, I realized that my disgust and hate for my seventeen-year-old self influenced my behavior toward her when she reached that age. It took that energy healing session for me to recognize how I had been keeping her at arm's length for some time. I wasn't as cuddly, fun, or playful with her as I once was. Without knowing it, I'd projected all my judgment and anger towards my younger self onto her.

In order to heal both my relationship with myself and my daughter, I needed to reclaim my scared and confused teenage self and bring her back to my body. Tell her how proud I was of her, love her, nurture her, and forgive her.

At one point in my healing journey I found myself at a womb ceremony. The process involved getting curious about how powerful our wombs are and the strength of what we as women can generate. It was a beautiful and cathartic release of everything I had held onto for so long. Movement of energy that had been stuck in my body for decades was finally released.

And then one day it happened. I felt that the seventeen year old version of myself came home. And as if I fully accepted her back into my body, I suddenly felt lighter and more whole. My body, which had carried the weight of that unhealed wound for decades, also began to change physically. The gut issues that had plagued me for years vanished, and the extra weight I carried in my lower abdomen started to melt away. It was then that I truly understood how deeply stuck energy can manifest in our bodies, how the emotional weight we carry can show up as physical symptoms, especially in the areas of our bodies tied to creation and birth. Reclaiming that lost piece of myself was the key to releasing both the emotional and physical burdens I had been carrying for so long.

I test my healing sometimes, through the newfound interaction with my daughter, hugging her, loving her, showering her with affection. It's in those moments that I know I've reclaimed a lost part of myself, and that I am whole.

Letting go and reclaiming my lost parts has also allowed me to completely level up in both my personal and professional life. It's allowed me to step into my true calling to bring others together in community, to amplify their voices, and to create platforms for collective impact. This calling—to serve humans—is my gift to the world and the reason for my presence on this Earth at this time. The journey to this realization was neither quick nor straightforward. It involved years of self-reflection, personal growth, and numerous encounters that shaped my understanding of service.

Often, we contemplate and discuss the multi-faceted aspects of womanhood. We are leaders, mothers, caregivers, nurturers, sisters, friends, daughters, and wives. These roles constitute the entirety of our being. However, we seldom delve into the moments in our lives when we may have given away a piece of ourselves, lost our power, or left a fragment of our hearts behind, or in my case, where pieces of ourselves died. These scattered pieces reside in different times, places, and spaces, shaped by our experiences. Each experience leaves its mark, influencing how we perceive ourselves and our roles in the world.

Through my personal journey, I've learned that growth often comes from the most challenging experiences. One of the most significant lessons learned through this work is the power of vulnerability. By opening up and sharing my story, and subsequently, my shame, it was inevitable that I would be able to create a space for connection and empathy. Vulnerability has allowed me to break down barriers and build genuine relationships based on trust and understanding. It is through vulnerability that I am ultimately able to inspire others and foster a sense of community.

Another important lesson I've learned is that serving others doesn't require perfection or complete healing. Growth and healing are continuous processes and can be done within a community. I've found that there is power in community, in witnessing one another, in belonging, accepting, and sharing in non-judgmental spaces.

Finally, a significant part of reclaiming my power came from reclaiming my voice. Sharing my once-shameful story openly and vulnerably diminished its hold over me. It enabled deeper connection and self-forgiveness.

The journey of self-discovery and healing is never truly complete. It is a continuous process of growth, learning, and evolution. Each day presents new opportunities to deepen our understanding of ourselves and the world around us. As we navigate this journey, I've found that it is important to remain open to change and embrace the lessons that come our way. When we do this, we learn to use our voices not only for ourselves but to open the door for healing for others. And for me, there's nothing more impactful than that. It's the ultimate embodiment of living a life of service.

ANITA PARKER

Anita Parker had a 26-year-long dental hygiene career before transitioning into entrepreneurship during the pandemic. She launched an online business, opened restaurants, and discovered her true passion in motivational speaking and philanthropy. Anita dedicates her time to empowering others internationally through events via a business she acquired and rebranded to Wisdom Wealth Well-Being. She brings individuals together to create community connections and belonging. Anita is a catalyst for turning passion into purpose and helps individuals in their personal and professional journeys to elevate and grow. She believes deeply in being of service to her community and locks arms with like-minded individuals to create a ripple effect into the world.

You can connect with Anita at anitaparkerbestlife@gmail.com or on Instagram at @anitabestlife or @wisdomwealthwellbeing.

I had a feeling in my heart that I was destined for more.

CHAPTER 16

From Small-Town Dreams to Beauty Brand Revolution

Missy MacKintosh

Growing up, I struggled with self-worth, not feeling like I belonged anywhere. I've always wondered if it was because I was a mid-life "oops" with parents who were married previously. They had two kids of their own, and had me by accident when my mom was thirty-nine and my dad was forty-three. At that time, in 1985, you were considered old to be having a baby at that point in your life.

I faced challenges of feeling accepted by both sides of my family. I felt like the black sheep, yearning for a happy connection with my family members but never truly feeling it. I had second cousins who were older than me, and the feeling of being an outsider weighed heavily on my heart. I wanted nothing more than a feeling of connection with both sides. I would try to be seen but often I felt out of place, and pushed aside.

Growing up as an only child on the outskirts of a small town, I felt the need to find things that brought me a sense of belonging. Makeup happened to be one of them. It was at the young age of three where my fascination began. My mom would find me tucked into a corner, blue crayons in hand, coloring on makeup to my dolls, with the biggest smile on my face. I would comment on actresses' makeup on TV, notice hair styles, and ask for makeup for Christmas because there was only ever one lipstick in our house, a Shiseido lipstick balm—I still remember the smell of it. Makeup lit a spark inside me and put a twinkle in my eye. It was art on a face. It had the ability to transform a person to be something completely different. Because my mom would not allow me to wear makeup, she bought me an easel and encouraged me to take my creative ability and paint on a flat canvas instead of face. You would find me hours on end painting whatever would flow while blasting Mariah Carey, in my basement bedroom. However it was not the same as painting on a 3-D canvas, and my obsession grew.

I was fourteen when my mom decided to join Mary Kay, and for a woman who embraced her natural side and natural remedies, this was a shock. We went from having just the one lipstick in the house to having Mary Kay products everywhere. I thought I died and went to heaven—there was finally makeup in my house. I became her right-hand girl for four years. We would lead parties, do makeup tutorials, and travel to conferences all across Canada. In fact, I was known as the Mary Kay Girl in high school. We would head off to the big city of Toronto for an annual conference. Small town girl in a big flashy city where dreams are made of. It was there that a thought came to me: *I don't just want to work for Mary Kay, I secretly want to BE Mary Kay, the one who is building a brand, formulating products, and empowering others.* But who does that? I live on the outskirts of a small town. Where dreams never happen. So, I put that thought in the back of my head.

When I was eighteen I was finally able to do Mary Kay on my own. My mom flew me to Dallas for a retreat, and there I met someone from the coast who told me she was going to school to become a makeup artist. My immediate thought was, "SHUT UP! You can do that?!" As soon as I got off the plane, I searched for makeup schools in Canada and found Blanche Macdonald. I hemmed and hawed over whether to take the esthetic course as I knew no one who had a career in makeup. But I took the risk and graduated with honors that following June and moved to Calgary right away with my high school sweetheart. I believed I could never follow my dream in a small town like Salmon Arm; the city was where I needed to be.

In Calgary, which is also my birth town, I worked for MAKE UP FOR EVER as a counter manager when I was twenty. It was a dream job and very rare back then, as MAKE UP FOR EVER would only hire artists already working in the industry. I was making it happen. This small town girl was doing something she never knew was possible—working in management for one of the most pristine makeup brands for professional makeup artists. Over time, I felt the need for a change and went to NARS. While living the makeup artist dream, I received a random call. I was personally headhunted by Shoppers Beauty Boutique to manage what was then the largest boutique in Western Canada and the first one to have MAKE UP FOR EVER. At twenty-one years old, I was one of their youngest managers in Canada.

Unfortunately, at the height of what I thought was going to be my career, one of my lowest moments in my life happened. We ended up having a silent miscarriage. After that experience, I wanted nothing more than my own family to love and create that sense of belonging that I yearned for when I was growing up. Losing the life growing inside me brought that desire for belonging back up within me right to the surface. So, I gave up my dream of city life and moved back to the small town of my childhood, Salmon Arm, so we could start a family. This moment confirmed that I will always be a small town girl at heart. A small town girl with big dreams. Dreams that I felt I had to give up in order for me to have a sense of belonging.

After my "big city" experience, I didn't want to work for the small town shoppers, so I pivoted and managed a travel agency for six years while we got married and had our son. A fiery entrepreneur at heart, I was going to buy the travel agency. But makeup followed me. I did the makeup for one wedding, and it snowballed to the point where I was working at it full-time while still managing the travel agency. Our son was two years old, and I was doing a wedding every single weekend. I had my first mental breakdown. I was trying so hard to fit in, have the family, the nine-to-five job, but something was missing. I had this big dream in my heart. A talent that I felt like was wasting away behind a computer. It was time to be honest about what I truly wanted to do with my life. I made the hard decision to quit my position at the agency and become a full-time freelance makeup artist. I was scared shitless. I was busy, but my income wasn't as steady as working for someone else. But I was determined to prove that I could make this happen.

I hustled, making connections with others in the industry, and doing free gigs to get my name out there. I was destined to prove to my family and myself that I can make this happen. I ended up working in Kelowna with full-time paying gigs. I worked with Opera Kelowna for three years as their lead artist creating and designing the looks, fashion campaigns, and commercials. I put together my own makeup artist training program, my work went viral multiple times with Cosmopolitan, Daily Mail, Huffington Post, and WedLuxe Magazine, and I got asked to help teach the makeup portion of the aesthetics program at Okanagan College in Vernon. I was also nominated for multiple awards during this time. I was feeling like I was on the top of the world. I took a chance on myself and it was working.

As great as everything was going in my career, I had a feeling in my heart that I was destined for more. This dream of having my own makeup brand was starting to come out of the shadows and into the forefront of my mind. As fate would have it, I was hired to do the campaign for Portia-Ella, a clean, green retailer, who retailed only Canadian-made brands, for their first store in Winnipeg. Back in 2016, no one was talking about clean beauty. At that point, I had studied airbrushing at the MAKE UP FOR EVER academy in Paris and was very much brand loyal to MAKE UP FOR EVER. I went into the first shoot, and sure enough, the products did not hold up to my professional, picky standards. However, they opened my eyes to how self-regulated this industry is and how many toxic ingredients were in everything. Once I went down the rabbit hole, I could not unsee it. I knew I needed to find products that were safer for myself and my clients, but trying to find what I was looking for didn't exist. I knew at that moment that MisMacK was ready to be here. MisMacK was an internet login I used back in the day, and I knew if I ever had my own makeup brand that is what it would be called. Through the power of manifestation, I found the most amazing female chemist in Manitoba, and she saw the vision and invested two years with me to perfect and build each product from the ground up.

From my basement in small-town, Canoe BC, I was set out to revolutionize the clean beauty world. I sourced everything from packaging to barcodes to building the website and branding. I didn't know anyone who had built a makeup brand before. Thankfully, my chemist helped as much as she could, but Google and I became best friends.

I was nervous, scared, almost ashamed of starting MisMacK from my basement. You see all these brands with big bright offices, in big cities, and it's just me in my basement located in no-one-has-ever-heard-of Canoe BC. Doubts constantly came into my head. *Who am I trying to be? Who do I think I am trying to build a brand? You're just a make-up artist. Small town people never make it.* All of this brought me back to the feeling I had when I thought I couldn't be in a small town to follow my dream as a makeup artist. I was afraid to start small. I was afraid of what others would think if it wasn't perfect. I'm a makeup artist; my work had to be perfect to be successful. My self worth at the time was based on what others thought of me.

I went through a lot of failures. I wanted MisMacK to be the first brand in Canada to offer an environmentally friendly glitter available at a retail level. And we were. We also launched GAIA Gloss as our first multi-use product that doubles as the primer for the glitters. Not knowing what you don't know until you do it, I sourced eco-friendly packaging. This included the lid to the GAIA, which was wider than the glitters. And every single one of those lids cracked on my customers. I was horrified. I wanted to recall them, my husband joked that people are going to start calling you "MisCrack." I put pride aside and was completely transparent, to the point that I printed, hand-cut little pieces of paper, and stuffed them in the GAIA boxes, which read, "Due to the eco-friendly nature of the plastic, please do not overturn your lid, or else it will crack on you." It was three years of my life saying this. We had clients duct-taping it, depotting GAIA, you name it. This crack in the lid reassured my negative thoughts that I am not worthy of creating a revolutionary brand. I was ashamed of putting something out to the world that wasn't perfect.

It was during the launch of our GlitterEnvi and GAIA at Portia-Ella Winnipeg where having no self-worth really came to the forefront. I had the ugliest of ugly-cry breakdowns. I'm talking about people staring at me at the mall Starbucks while I was waiting for my pumpkin-spiced latte with thoughts of self-doubt flooding my head and tears running down my face. It was at this moment, as I was walking back to Portia-Ella, coffee in hand, eyes swollen, nose dripping, where one of their staff came running up to me saying CBC Radio just called and they want me in their studio for a live interview during rush hour to talk about MisMacK. This moment changed everything for me. This little small town girl was about to be live on air with CBC Radio in Winnipeg to talk about the brand SHE is building.

While eco glitter was great in theory, it was a huge flop. Turns out glitter is one of the hardest sales in the cosmetics industry. It's pretty and we all love looking at it, but it's very intimidating to use as a consumer. I knew we needed to get the makeup that we'd been developing out into the world. My dad invested in me to help make our first launch happen and invested again to help me launch our makeup collection.

On May 10th, 2019, ten foundations, one setting powder, sixteen ART shadows, one magnetic palette, and seven shades of lipstick officially came into the world under the MisMacK brand. At that point, I was focused on what other brands were doing on the wholesale side of their business. Asking myself how they were getting their products on the shelves of other businesses, because that's what everyone does. I was trying to fit in, and we were barely keeping afloat. I felt I was building other people's businesses while learning the business of MisMacK. Then in March 2020, we all know what happened, exactly two weeks after being a finalist for the BC Small Business Awards for Best Youth Entrepreneur, the world shut down.

Having the world shut down, and of course, all my retailers, gave me permission to go direct to the consumer. Within that first week of lockdown, I offered online Zoom lessons, giving me the opportunity to connect with others while being stuck at home. The following week I had people from Boston, Toronto, and Winnipeg joining, which boosted our online sales. I donated five dollars from every ticket sold to our local food bank in Salmon Arm.

Once things started to open back up, I lost most of my retailers. Which I totally get; makeup is not a passive sale, where the product sells itself on the shelf. People started to come to my basement to shop, do lessons, and do bridal hair and makeup trials. I was teaching my course out of my basement, which was great, but it was time to take the next step of finding our own location.

My skincare chemist, who I worked with in Salmon Arm to create our best-selling skincare, messaged me on the day I was looking for the perfect home for MisMacK. She told me she was moving to Saskatchewan and hopes that I will still want to work with her. I said, "Of course! And I'm going to take over your lease." It's the perfect little location in downtown Salmon Arm.

We opened the doors to our Salmon Arm location on April 10th, 2021, with COVID rules fully in effect of having only five people in the shop at a time (wild to look back on), everyone wearing masks, and all the protocols followed. Because I know makeup is not a passive sale and HATE the word makeover, I created our signature free pampering sessions. These pampering sessions made MisMacK sales soar.

We did so well that I opened my second location five months later in Victoria. It was a beautiful location downtown. I thought this was it, we hit the jackpot. If we were doing so well in Salmon Arm, imagine what Victoria would bring. After signing another two-year lease, we showed up to our shop with our sidewalk storefronts blocked off by the city with no warning to any of the businesses located there. With no communication as to how long the sidewalk would be blocked off, all we could do was keep a positive outlook and try to move forward. This was entirely out of our hands. That same year, MisMacK Victoria took home Bronze for Community Votes Victoria for the best Cosmetics Store in 2022. It was amazing to receive this recognition from the community of Victoria within our first year of opening despite the setbacks. This reassured me that I made the right decision with opening up Victoria.

Life outside of business had other plans for me. That summer, my dad's health deteriorated, and he was diagnosed with dementia. After being in the hospital for weeks, his health needs were beyond my family's capabilities at home. I found him a new home in an assisted living facility. My goal was to make sure his room felt like home, and my mom (they divorced when I was 18) helped me get his house ready for the market. Needless to say, my mind was focused on him and his health and not as much on the business and my own small family. My relationship with my dad switched from him being my parent to me parenting him. It broke my heart. My focus was not on MisMacK but on my dad because it was phone call after phone call of him falling and ending up back in the hospital.

A new location in Kelowna had been on my vision board for two years. This is where I built my freelance career. I knew it was the next move for a MisMacK location. During the hardest part of taking care of my dad, a dear friend reached out to me saying they wanted to invest in a MisMacK store with me. It was such a breath of fresh air and the light at the end of this dark tunnel. I told my dad, and he was beyond excited. He would ask me every day if MisMacK Kelowna had opened. I told him no, it wasn't meant to be.

Christmas came that year and it was the first Christmas in over five years that my dad joined us on Christmas Day. It was amazing to see his smile and to hear his laughter with our family again. That week he ended up back in the hospital. I picked him up on New Year's Day to take him back to his place at an assisted living facility, and it was the first time he called it home. The following weekend I took him to our son's two hockey games. He was loving life. He ate two whole hot dogs and a huge bag of popcorn in one sitting. I felt the happiness in his heart.

The Tuesday morning after that weekend, I noticed the morning sky was intensely pink. Within twenty minutes, I got a call from my dad's assisted living facility stating my dad had a fall, and they couldn't say anything more. Ten minutes later, I got a call from his doctor, who happened to be working in the emergency room that morning. He told me my dad had a fatal fall and was not going to make it. I rushed down and almost dropped to my knees seeing him on the bed in a coma. My life at that moment shattered.

My biggest fan and supporter passed away that afternoon. My whole life shrank. All my insecurities from growing up and feeling all alone came rushing back to me. My sense of belonging was gone. It spun me into a very dark place for months where I questioned even moving forward with MisMacK.

During my darkest days, I kept seeing an ad for UPLIFT Women's Business Summit where Jamie Kern Lima, the founder of IT Cosmetics, was the keynote speaker. Jamie is one of my all-time idols. When I started MisMacK, someone sent me her book Believe IT and told me I'm like the next Jamie Kern Lima. She started her company in her living room, and I started mine in my basement. She ended up having the biggest acquisition in L'Oréal's history of 1.2 billion dollars and was the first female CEO sitting on the board of L'Oréal in 2017. I absolutely adore her, and her story gave me the strength to build MisMacK. This ad kept popping up as if it was my dad saying you need to be there. Sure enough, the event was mere blocks from my Victoria location. I invested some of my inheritance to be a platinum sponsor for the event that November.

But Kelowna kept calling. After hearing about Portia-Ella closing their Kelowna location, a gap in the market opened up. During the depths of my grieving time, I told myself that I wouldn't open any new stores for two years. Well, my dad had other plans. On Father's Day 2023, the first Father's Day without my dad, something told me to look at the MLS listings in Kelowna. I couldn't believe it; the most perfect location was available. A small unit attached to the outside of the Delta Hotels Grand Okanagan Resort. I knew my dad was giving me a sign, and he would want me to invest my inheritance into a Kelowna store. I didn't hesitate. I jumped on this opportunity and submitted an offer. I got the keys a few months later. Having the keys in my hands to my dream location was a moment I will never forget. Not only was this location incredibly special, this store was being built in honor of my Dad. The Kelowna location was ready in just three weeks.

But Mother Nature had other plans. We were supposed to open the Tuesday after the fire jumped the Okanagan Lake, which was in the midst of the devastation of the Shuswap fires. It was wild. We had to postpone the opening.

MisMacK Kelowna eventually opened in September 2023, and that November at UPLIFT, I had the most successful two days of MisMacK's history. I was the only person who had the opportunity to meet Jamie Kern

Lima. She was so incredibly kind, she took me up on stage to listen whole-heartedly to my story. She asked me if I had ever thought about the shopping channel. I certainly had, but when asked if I had a contact there I told her I didn't. "Do you want one?" Um... YES! She told me to pitch my business into her phone and that she was going to send it to her contact that helped her get started. In a matter of fifteen minutes, I had never felt more seen in my entire life. The next day at the UPLIFT Women's Business Summit, I had the honor of doing Canada's beloved body positive influencer, Sarah Nicole Landry's, known online as Birds Papaya, makeup and shared my story for the first time unapologetically in a breakout room. From that, we had the biggest sales at the booth in the company's history.

Little did I know that in the height of this success, we were about to embark into the hardest winter of MisMacK's history and the closure of our storefront in Victoria, then straight into one of the highest of the highs. Alongside my son, we launched Game Play Eye Black, Canada's first ever toxic-free eye black for sports. We pitched our little hearts out on the set of Dragon's Den together and got GamePlay into the hands of the Blue Jays.

And that's where my story finds us today with yet untold adventures ahead..

See, I believe everything happens for a reason. If I didn't have the fail of our GAIA Gloss lid, it would have never gotten the glow-up that you see today. I believe you have to fail into your flow. It's in these moments of struggle that our true course is charted. You must start small to go tall, even if the "small" is your basement in your tiny town. Each small step is a critical part of the journey, building strength and resilience as you climb. And never, ever be ashamed of having big, audacious dreams—no matter how out of this world they may seem, or how humble your beginnings. Whether you're starting out in a small town basement or a bustling city corner, your dreams are valid and possible. Embrace them. Own them. Because no one else will build your dream for you. It's on you to put in the work, to believe when others doubt, and to push forward when hard obstacles come your way. And they will, believe me. So dream big, start small, and rise tall. Your potential is limitless, and your path is yours alone to pave.

MISSY MACKINTOSH

Missy MacKintosh is an internationally acclaimed makeup artist and fiery entrepreneur. Missy founded and built Canada's most award-winning clean beauty brand, MisMacK Clean Cosmetics in her small town of Canoe BC. She single-handedly grew out of her basement and into two storefronts during a global pandemic.

Recently named Most Influential Business Leaders to Follow in Canada by Insight Success Magazine and Top 50 One's to Watch Keynote Speakers in the Real Leaders Magazine.

You can find Missy at www.mismack.com, @missymackintosh on all socials, or send her an email at missy@mismack.com

Through a lens of compassion, I've been able to come back to the most authentic version of myself.

CHAPTER 17

On the Other Side of the Bottle

Alex Vigue

Freedom. That's what I felt the first time Drunk Alex came crashing into my life. It was at a party in a field behind my friend's house on the last day of school in grade nine.

At the far end of the field, an intimidating group of football players were doing keg stands. I never would have talked to them at school, let alone at a party with so many people watching. But, on this particular day, I'd had one beer and was feeling brave. So I turned to my friend and said, "I'm doing it."

I walked over, sauntered really, with a new-found liquid courage I'd eventually come to know so well, and stood arms crossed in front of the hottest player.

"I'll do one," I said, nodding toward the keg.

"Ever done one," his buddy asked

"Nope," I answered.

They looked at each other, shrugged and then after a brief rundown, told me to grab the sides and hoisted my legs up. A crowd cheered, counting down from thirty, beer spilling everywhere at the end.

In that moment I felt something I'd never felt before—a rush of freedom and a deep rooted sense of belonging. It's that feeling, and the relentless pursuit to recreate it, that became the catalyst for a two decade toxic relationship with a drunken version of myself.

My relationship with Drunk Alex wasn't always toxic. In the beginning she was a breath of fresh air, freeing me temporarily and sporadically from the inner critic that plagued my mind.

Where I repressed, she expressed. And unlike my tendency to

165

hesitate, Drunk Alex never held back. What seemed to fuel Drunk Alex, was her mission to prove to the world that she was enough—fun enough, pretty enough, cool enough, and just a little crazy enough to get noticed. There was something I loved about her uninhibited wildness which led me to cling tightly to her side.

Because of that, Drunk Alex was there for so many moments in my life; my first real kiss, the first time I let a guy feel me up, and the first time I walked down the stairs of a house I shared with friends determined to have sex for the first time with some random guy I'd picked up at the Blarney Stone in Vancouver.

I can still see my friend standing at the top of the stairs as I skipped down in a pleated mini jean skirt, black crop top, and knee high boots. Ever the pragmatist, she took a minute before asking,

"Are you sure this is what you want?

"Yes, don't worry about it!" I replied.

Then I hopped into a car with the guy and let Drunk Alex take over drinking beers at the bar before completing our task.

"How was it?" the guy, Dan, I think his name was, asked the next morning.

"Okay," I said, desperately trying to remember the whole experience.

"Just okay?!" he replied, dismissively.

"Yeah," I said, embarrassed that I couldn't remember what was supposed to be a pivotal moment in my life.

"Well, I guess we're done then," he said. I nodded, the shame settling in as he drove me home in silence. The entire car ride, I couldn't shake the feeling that I'd done or said something wrong or that maybe he'd realized I wasn't that attractive after all. Without the liquid courage, I immediately felt ashamed of never being enough.

Shame and not-enoughness were never issues for Drunk Alex. And this I quickly realized was one of her problems. Because, in her attempt to prove our worthiness to me, Drunk Alex sometimes went a little too far. Free from the shackles of self doubt, it was like all she wanted to do was ride more of that high.

It's in those moments that Drunk Alex would take risks I didn't approve of in the light of the morning. Like the time in university when she left the bar and hitchhiked home in the back of a pickup truck. The next day I remember feeling an overwhelming sense of dread when I thought about how I could have been raped or left in a ditch to die.

Which is why, after university, I vowed not to let Drunk Alex get too wild and gave her rules around drinking. She could only drink on the weekends. She could have three drinks, four maximum, at any event. Most importantly, she couldn't drink if she felt emotional because then all she'd do is cry.

And for a long time my rules worked. But, every now and then Drunk Alex would tow that wild line again and I'd wake up in my bed fully clothed with my boots on trying desperately to remember the details of how I got there.

For the most part though, Drunk Alex seemed under control until October of 2009, when I got H1N1 and had my capital T trauma moment and ended up on life support. Tired and weak from spending six months in the hospital, it took a while for Drunk Alex to resurface again.

In those early days of re-assimilating into non-hospital life, I felt void of all emotion. Apathy plagued me and I walked around on autopilot, desperate to feel something—anything, for a moment. Then a party would happen and Drunk Alex would step in and I'd feel it again—joy. Even if the feeling was fleeting, I loved Drunk Alex for giving me that.

Drunk Alex stayed in her joy-giving phase for years. During the early stages of motherhood she loved mom playdates with wine, and trick-or-treating with a Yeti cooler. And, in this particular phase of her existence, Drunk Alex provided me with friendship and camaraderie and made it easy to ignore and stuff down any feelings of unhappiness I had.

And then one day it happened. Drunk Alex began her slow spiral down from joyful and fun to mean and reckless. It was on a summer day out day-drinking with a friend, where Drunk Alex unleashed every feeling I'd bottled so tightly inside. Maybe I didn't love my husband, Drunk Alex professed. Maybe I had married him out of obligation, maybe I wanted something different, maybe it was time to consider something else. It all came pouring out.

That night, fueled by her bold need to speak my truth, Drunk Alex went home and told my husband she didn't think I loved him and that I thought we were heading for divorce. I can still see Drunk Alex crying on a pink bean bag chair in the sunroom confessing it all.

I wish I could remember exactly what she said, but like so many of those uninhibited moments, I can only remember snippets. What I do know is that her confession permanently changed the dynamic of my marriage. Drunken words spewed that I could never take back.

And believe me I tried. But the thing about suppressing feelings is that they always come to the surface. Always. And the more I pushed them down, the more Drunk Alex became deeply entangled in my existence, so much so that one day she took over and I couldn't reign her back. All the pieces of my own identity lost.

In the five years that followed the day on the pink bean bag chair there were many shame-filled moments that I tried to reconcile with. I lied. I cheated. I passed out in front of my children, and told my husband that I wished he would die more times than I can count.

And more often than not, I'd wake up thinking this would be the last time I'd cause chaos. I'd get Drunk Alex under control again. But, she was no longer within my grasp. And she seemed desperate to tell the world how unhappy I was, no matter the cost.

In this phase of her existence, Drunk Alex could drink a bottle of wine in less than an hour and needed to open another to feel those blissful moments of escape that used to come so easily. She drank to pass out most days, sometimes in the bathtub where she would have to be hoisted out by her husband. And in the light of the morning, the shame of Drunk Alex's words and actions became so unbearable that it felt like the only relief came the second I opened another bottle.

Still, despite knowing she was a problem, I couldn't shake her. I tried taking a thirty-day no drinking challenge here and there, even an eighty-day break once during COVID. But Drunk Alex kept coming back determined to unleash everything I'd ever felt.

Then one day she imploded, and, in a drunken argument with my husband she watched him pour the rest of her wine down the sink. Angry and frustrated, she hit him. I wish I could remember her doing it but I can't. The only evidence were scratches on my husband and a drunken recording where she sounded crazed.

The consequences of those actions were permanent. An arrest and the final dissolution of my marriage. But still, I clung tightly to Drunk Alex's side.

Until one weekend away in Vegas with friends, Drunk Alex's shadow came out into the light of day. Passing out in the hotel hot tub, shitting herself in the hotel room, and permanently damaging friendships in the process.

I flew home from that trip broken, mostly because I knew that I couldn't hide Drunk Alex from anyone anymore, including myself, and knowing that even though I didn't want to, I finally needed to set her free.

Sometimes I miss her. Not the reckless version she became, but the wild uninhibited freedom-seeker she once was. The life of the party who was always up for a good time, and the sweet feeling of relief I'd get when she'd take over and all my worries and self doubt would instantly melt away.

Still, for everything I miss about Drunk Alex, there are thousands of things I don't. In breaking free from her grasp, I've gained a deep sense of inner peace. One that's led me to find forgiveness for the reckless and hurtful version of myself she eventually became. And, in letting her go through a lens of compassion, I've been able to come back to the most authentic version of myself. That process has been a gift. One that's led me to feel brighter, bolder, and happier than I can ever remember feeling. Ultimately, it's given me a powerful sense of freedom. Which is everything I spent years chasing and was never able to hold on to while walking in Drunk Alex's shadow on the other side of the bottle.

ALEX VIGUE

Alex is an entrepreneur, mom, speaker, writer, and co-host of the Let's Not Sugarcoat It Podcast. After a two decade roller-coaster relationship with booze, she embarked on a journey to discover what life looks like on the other side of the bottle. Alex's passion lies in helping others share their stories and voices with the world. Known for bearing her darkest truths in public, she hopes that in revealing her most vulnerable moments of shame, she can help inspire others to step into their most authentic self and reach whatever it is they're striving to achieve on the other side of what's holding them back.

Find her on letsnotsugarcoatit.com or connect on Instagram at @lets.not.sugarcoat.it.podcast and @ontheothersideofthebottle.

Take each step with faith and courage.

CHAPTER 18

Standing Up, Stepping Out: How Faith and Courage Shaped My Success

Samantha Wedlund

As a child, I was bullied relentlessly by this one girl in particular. For six years she made fun of me, taunted me, and got others on board to join in the bullying. She pulled my hair and hit me; the bullying was both physical and emotional. Therefore, a defining moment in my life was when I finally stood up to her. As the school chanted "*fight, fight, fight,*" I suddenly found the inner strength to defend myself. And though physical confrontation is not always the right path, that moment taught me to take my power back.

The bullying started in kindergarten when we moved, and I had to wear a different uniform. In Jamaica, uniforms symbolize community. Mine was a different color because we couldn't afford a new one after moving, making me stick out like a sore thumb. It screamed, "You don't belong," and made me the perfect target for bullying that continued until that day on the playground six years later.

All throughout most of my childhood, I'd been a timid spirit—shy, quiet, and wrestling with feelings of abandonment after my father left at a young age. As a result, I never felt like I fit in and thought of myself as an outcast. My experience at school amplified those feelings.

But that moment on the playground changed everything. Even though I was smaller and quieter, I pushed back, and instantly gained a tremendous amount of respect by my peers. After that fight, I was never bullied again. It felt like a pendulum swinging the other way, and suddenly I was revered by others. Each of us has a story that has shaped our view of the world and defined who we've become and the work that we do. My experiences as a child taught me resilience, but not without a cost. Because on that day, I ended the bullying, but soon became a bully myself.

That experience on the playground taught me that when you stand up for yourself, you gain respect. This eventually led me to own my own salon as an adult, a space where I help women feel beautiful when they look in the mirror, and even when they don't. There is much more depth to my work than just outward beauty.

My salon is a place where people open their hearts, share their stories, and reveal their dreams. I like to think of it as a support center for all areas of life. It's a space where people come to be seen and heard. For me, the most important gift I offer others is the ability to help see themselves for who they truly are and to take a chance on their dreams. I love teaching others that they can stand up for themselves, just like I did.

But before I got to this place, I had to learn some hard lessons. That moment on the playground where I found my voice also had its downsides because I turned that voice against others. I became the bully. People were scared of me. I got into trouble, and my mother didn't know what to do with me. I was constantly talking back, getting into fights, and my name was always being called over the school loudspeakers.

Then, in high school, I started playing dangerous games, as we say in Jamaica. I was in texting relationships with multiple guys, staying out late after school with girlfriends, and hurting those I love with my actions 'trying to fit in'. One day, when I was fifteen, I saw my mom crying. I asked her, "Why are you crying? Do you not like me as a daughter?" I didn't understand why she was so disappointed. I thought I was showing her love—I would write her the best love letters—but I couldn't see how my behavior was hurting her. In that moment it became clear to me that I gave my mother a lot of grief in my mission to stand up for everyone.

So, at fifteen, tired of feeling bad and disappointing my mother. I decided to make a change. I went to church and asked, *"Can the God we serve here do something about my attitude?"* The pastor replied, *"He's the only one who can."* So I took a leap and got baptized, and through reading the Bible, I became a brand-new person. It was as though I had been given a clean slate and a new lease on life.

After that, things started to unfold for the better. My mom challenged me to become one of the top three students in high school. Not to compete with others, but to be the best I could be. Her challenge inspired me to work hard, and I achieved many awards, but more than that, I discovered the power of self-discipline.

At twenty years old, I moved from Jamaica to Canada to take a chance on my dreams. I applied for accounting jobs without success but found my place in a hair studio. After working at the hair studio and a hotel, my husband and I desired to have a child. When I found myself pregnant with our first son, returning to work didn't feel right. So, I took another chance on myself and started my salon in our one-bedroom apartment. What started small has now grown into a successful business with a team of seven and a storefront.

Starting my salon in a one-bedroom apartment was a leap of faith, and it wasn't easy. There were days of doubt and fear, but I kept moving forward, fueled by faith and determination. My little salon grew, and with it, so did my faith. I saw God's hand in every step, every challenge, and every victory. Building a team of seven and moving to a storefront was a dream come true. Each person who joined my team brought their unique strengths and stories. Together, we created a space where clients felt loved, valued, and beautiful. We became more than just a salon; we became a community.

Looking back, I see how every struggle, every challenge, and every triumph was part of God's plan to mold me into who I am today. My story is a testament to the power of faith, resilience, and the willingness to take a chance on oneself. It is a reminder that with God, all things are possible.

I am grateful to my younger self for fighting for what was right and embracing her differences. These differences became my strengths and set me apart on my path to success. I thank her every day for betting on herself because that's what I want for every woman who sits in my chair at the salon—to take a chance on themselves and their dreams.

My faith in God has guided me through these journeys, providing strength and direction. Believing in God has helped me see my worth and potential, reminding me that with faith, anything is possible. Through each challenge, I leaned on God's promises, and specific scriptures became my anchor, helping me navigate the ups and downs of life.

Deuteronomy 8:18 says, *"But remember the Lord your God, for it is he who gives you the ability to produce wealth, and so confirms his covenant, which he swore to your ancestors, as it is today."* This scripture has been a cornerstone in my life, especially during challenging times. It continuously reminds me that God has given me the power to create wealth and to achieve my dreams.

Let's Not Sugarcoat It

Growing up, my mindset was heavily influenced by Philippians 4:8, which states, *"Finally, brothers and sisters, whatever is true, whatever is noble, whatever is right, whatever is pure, whatever is lovely, whatever is admirable—if anything is excellent or praiseworthy—think about such things."* This scripture helped me focus on positive thoughts and kept me grounded, even when circumstances were tough.

Another scripture that has provided me with immense comfort is Psalm 91:4: *"He will cover you with his feathers, and under his wings, you will find refuge; his faithfulness will be your shield and rampart."* Knowing that God's protection is always with me has given me the courage to face adversities head-on.

Reflecting on these scriptures, I see how they shaped my journey. When I moved to Canada, leaving behind everything familiar, I clung to my faith. It wasn't just about starting a new life; it was about trusting God's plan for me. Despite the initial struggles and rejections in the accounting field, I found solace in my passion for cosmetology.

At the hair salon, I learned more than just the craft of hairstyling. I learned the importance of connection, listening, and offering support. Clients would often share their deepest fears and greatest hopes. In those moments, I realized that my work was a ministry. I was not only transforming their appearance but also their self-perception. When I decided to start my salon, it was a leap of faith. I remember praying and seeking God's guidance. Proverbs 3:5-6 says, *"Trust in the Lord with all your heart and lean not on your own understanding; in all your ways submit to him, and he will make your paths straight."* This scripture reassured me that my path would become clear as long as I trusted in God.

My life has been a journey of faith, resilience, and self-belief. The scriptures have been my guiding light, providing wisdom, strength, and protection. As I continue to grow and evolve, I hold onto the promise that God has given me the power to create wealth, the wisdom to focus on what is good, and the assurance of His protection.

To every reader, I encourage you to take a chance on yourself. Embrace your unique journey, trust in God's plan, and know that you have the power within you to achieve greatness. As Jeremiah 29:11 says, *"For I know the plans I have for you,"* declares the Lord, *"plans to prosper you and not to harm you, plans to give you hope and a future."*

Believe in those plans, and take each step with faith and courage.

SAMANTHA WEDLUND

Samantha Wedlund is an award-winning entrepreneur, wife, mother of three, educator and visionary, owning the award-winning Success 21 Salon, where she empowers women to feel confident and beautiful through hair extensions and personal transformation. With a passion for financial independence, she teaches others to achieve their dreams and reach their full potential. Samantha's faith in God and resilience have shaped her journey, guiding her to success in both life and business. To connect with Samantha further, follow her on LinkedIn: Samantha Wedlund, Instagram at @Samanthawedlund1 or @Success21Salon for inspiration and updates on her latest ventures.

Email: info@success21salon.com Contact: 250-681-0436

The Dark Night of the Soul

A single bullet to the right temple of his head
A harrowing, deadly scream from his wife and best friend
Fucking nothing left to be said
A gold medal dental surgeon dead
Witnessing this act...to the closet she fled
Wondering was it something she said
A storybook life they both had led
So deeply in love just newly wed
Now, she's reeling with anger and seeing red
How, why is he lying there dead
No goodbye, no why
Warning signs were not read
She's spinning in pain now paralyzed in a psychiatric bed
Left alone, abandoned her soul cannot be fed

No one comprehends the life she just shed
Losing her best friend, needing him back she pled
She took her own life, found by a thread
Woke three days later to see her mom's heart...bled
Coming back from this journey her heart might not mend
Starting National Suicide Awareness now it will end.

Dhorea Ramanula

Acknowledgements

To those who have ever felt invisible in their pain, this chapter is a testament to the power of resilience and the light that exists within, even in your darkest moments. - *Carien Rennie*

To Drunk Alex; I love you, I forgive you, and now it's time to set you free. - *Alex Vigue*

I dedicate this chapter to my dad, the original superhero in my life—who has always loved and supported me. I wish you could see this next badass version of me, though I can already see you at the kitchen table rolling your eyes at some of crazy ideas. I miss you more than you can imagine. Love you forever! - *Izabela Picco*

To the little one whose journey was brief, you are deeply loved and will always hold a special place in my heart. Your presence, though fleeting, has left an everlasting impact. - *Anita Parker*

To my children who without them would not have realized dreams I never knew were possible. - *Lisa Moore*

I dedicate this chapter to my Dad, my greatest supporter, whose love and belief in me continue to guide me from above and to my incredible family who have stood beside me through every high and low—your strength, love, and unwavering support empower me every day. - *Missy MacKintosh*

To my son who has given me a new lease on life and self-love and to all those who have left this earth from suicide, mental health and addiction—we see you and miss you! - *Dhorea Ramanula*

To my beautiful daughter, Rylah Doucet, granddaughter Payton Doucet, and my two boys Aaiden and Grayson. - *Chantaal Doucet*

To my kids, I love you more than life itself. - *Brett Phillips*

To my younger, inexperienced, and ever so naive self. - *Crystelle Gordon*

I dedicate my story to my parents, Terry and Lance Roberts—You have been a wonderful source of support and inspiration and taught me to reach for the stars, follow my dreams, and to always believe in myself.
- *Shannan Roberts*

For my parents, whose unwavering love and support have shaped the person I am today, and to my beautiful daughters, the light of my life, your strength and spirit inspire me every day. - *Heidi Johnson*

For the healthcare workers fighting silently and in memory of those who lost the battle. Don't forget, you matter too. - *Paige Mathison*

This chapter is dedicated to my mum, Sandra Bearss, who recently went through a long battle with breast cancer; I am in absolute awe of her strength, her attitude and commitment to life. - *Erica Bearss*

This is dedicated to all the young women who feel lost and need to be found.
- *Ania Trimble*

Dedicated to my beautiful, strong mother, whose unwavering strength and love have been my greatest inspiration. - *Sanela Sehovac*

To my husband Cass, my love, my one and only - thank you for always inspiring me to share our story. To our children Briar, Vale and Riddick - without you, there would be no story to tell. I love you all beyond measure.
- *Kathryn Morrow*

This chapter is dedicated to my mother, for always investing in me, and is my biggest cheerleader, to my family for their continuous inspiration and love poured into me, and to my pastors for their mentorship and dedication to me. I thank God for each of you, and I hope you are blessed as you read this chapter. - *Samantha Wedlund*

Author Listing

Carien Rennie
Instagram: @carienrennie

Alex Vigue
Instagram: @lets.not.sugarcoat.it.podcast

Izabela Picco
Email: info@letsnotdugarcoatit.com

Anita Parker
Instagram: @anitabestlife

Lisa Moore
Email: lisa.crossroadscollective@gmail.com

Missy MacKintosh
Instagram: @missymackintosh

Dhorea Ramanula
Instagram: @Dhorea08

Chantaal Doucet
Instagram: @chantaaldoucet

Brett Phillips
www.naturopathichealthcare.ca

Crystelle Gordon
Instagram: @bodybarkelowna

Shannan Roberts
Instagram: @thejoyofhumanconnection

Heidi Johnson
Instagram: @heidi.johnson21

Paige Mathison
Instagram: @detraumatizinghealthcare

Erica Bearss
LinkedIn: www.linkedin.com/in/ericabearssmba

Ania Trimble
Instagram: @balanceholisticnutrition.yeg

Sanela Sehovac
Instagram: @carpediemtourskelowna

Sam Wedlund
Instagram: @samanthawedlund1

Kathryn Morrow
Instagram: @kathrynmorrowonline

About Let's Not Sugarcoat It

At Let's Not Sugarcoat It, our mission is to move, touch, and inspire others through genuine, unfiltered, and honest conversations. We believe that by sharing our own experiences and engaging in vulnerable discussions, we can forge deep connections, create a truly human experience, and have a profound impact on community and people around the world.

Our podcast was born out of a passion to have real, raw, and unfiltered conversations about life's most vulnerable moments, struggles, and challenges This book is an extension of our podcast designed to give others a platform to share and connect through storytelling.

Find out more at: www.letsnotsugarcoatit.com, over on Instagram @lets.not.sugarcoat.it.podcast, or email us at info@letsnotsugarcoatit.com

Made in United States
Troutdale, OR
10/08/2024